I0840708

A Cup of Tea

By: Paul Toritto 28 December 2024

What we have lost . . . May not have

been lost at all.

The End

This book is the culmination of twelve years of
work on the Abby Woo series, none of which
would have been possible without the love,
inspiration, and support of my wonderful wife,

Barbara Ann Toritto.

Partners in Life.

Love you Forever!

Body Count

"Hey, DeLuca, it's Richards. Give me a call ASAP. It's about the body count at Pennville. I told you and that country bumpkin of a marshal, God rest her soul, that something smelt like shit." Richards thought for a moment about the man he had recently befriended and then added more words to the voice mail message. "Seriously, Paolo, this is important. Call me as soon as you get this."

When Detective Richards disconnected the phone, he threw it onto his desktop inbox. It sat there most of the time along with his important but otherwise forgotten casefiles. One item in the final report of the Franklin Bank robbery and the aftermath at Pennville Asylum was bugging the hell out of him; the final body count was off by one. His captain had ordered him to review the file today with a few choice words to motivate the detective. "I need the fucking thing signed by COB, Richards. Peruse it and sigh the damn thing, will you?"

Richards was not one to be left without the last word. "Nice big word you used there, Captain—peruse." He had said, exaggerating the vowels for effect. "Did you look that up in your policeman's thesaurus? You ever realize you have a propensity to use prodigious words when you want to get your point across, you jackass paper-pushin' motherfucker?"

Richards hadn't seen the discrepancy in the body count until his boss had made him review the report for the third time. He referred to his field notebook just in case he was mistaken, but he knew he wasn't. After he left another message for DeLuca, he took the paperwork into the captain's office in a bit of an exaggerated huff. He didn't care the door was closed and that the captain was in a meeting with another detective. He did as he always did, walked straight in without knocking and started talking.

"I'm not signing off on this shit." Richards threw the paper file on the man's desk exaggerating his disdain for the task.

"You see I'm in a meeting here, Richards?" the captain asked in a rhetoric tone.

"With this joker?" He panned from Detective Owens to the captain, as if asking the question wasn't also rhetorical.

Owens started mouthing off to Richards, but, when Richards looked him in the eye, he made some excuse and left the office. Richards was a foot taller and about a hundred pounds heavier than Owens; it wouldn't have been a fair fight.

"What the hell is wrong with it now, Richards? Christ, the case is old news already. Sign the friggin' thing, so I can close it out. We have other cases to solve, Detective."

"The goddamn body count is wrong, Watts! Who the fuck changed the count?"

"You were overwhelmed that day, Richards. You could have easily miscounted the damn bodies. Lord knows you and DeLuca left enough of them lying around the Pennville grounds!"

Richards opened the casefile facing the captain as it sat on his desk. He flipped through each page that contained a photo and a rap sheet of each of the dead criminals at the bank and at Pennville. He slammed his index finger onto each photo after flipping each page, and he accentuated each finger thump on the desk with one word, "Male!" It went something like this, Flip, thump, "Male." Flip, thump, "Male." Flip, thump, "Male"

"Alright, alright, Richards, I get it. All the fucking dead guys are male. Jesus Christ!"

"Exactly!"

"Exactly? What the fuck do you mean, exactly, Richards?" Am I missing something here?"

Richards didn't understand why he had to point out the obvious. After all, Watts knew this case just as well as Richards did. He knew about the bound between Richards and DeLuca and about DeLuca's girlfriend Abby.

"Where's the dame female victim's body? How come she's the only dead guy not in the report?"

"How the hell am I supposed to know where the body is? Ask the goddamn coroner."

"I ain't signing that shit, Captain. Not until I know where her body is."

"What the fuck difference does one body make, Richards? If the coroner said they collected twenty-one bodies. Twenty-two ain't gonna make a damn bit of difference in the report."

"That twenty-second body was important, Captain. She was the twin sister of Abby Woo. Now how the hell am I supposed to tell Woo and DeLuca that the coroner lost the sister's body?"

"You're too close to this shit, Richards. This DeLuca Woo thing almost cost you your badge, and that trip to Texas you took without authorized leave, that's what got you the three days off without pay. Sign the fucking report or give me your badge and your service weapon!"

Richards wanted to continue the argument, but it would be futile. He grabbed the file, flipped to the last page and scribbled what passed for his signature on all of his official documents—a capital M followed by a capitol R with a squiggly line after it. It no more looked like the name Michael Richards than a kindergartener's mark with a black crayon.

When Richards returned to his desk, his cellphone was chiming a soft bell tone, indicating he had a message waiting. He checked the screen and realized DeLuca had called while he and the captain were arguing about the damn file.

Richards hit Redial, and Paolo answered on the first ring. "What's up?"

Normally Richards was well spoken, but, when he was mad—infuriated like he was now—his Philly—street dialect slipped out in full display. "These motherfuckers got me fumin' over this final fuckin' report. Wanting me to sign shit I ain't agreein' wit'. Wantin' me to agree to shit I don't agree with. Wantin' me to cover up shit I know is a fuckin' lie!"

"What are you talking about, Richards?" Paolo tried not to laugh at the colorful outburst.

Richards realize he hadn't told Paolo that Abby's sister's body was missing from the morgue and calmed himself. "Sorry, Paolo. I need to tell you something I'm finding particularly hard to understand."

"What is it, Michael?"

Richards thought it best just to lay it out there. "Abby's sister's body, it's missing from the morgue and from the official report."

"Shit! Abby just made arrangements with a funeral home for them to retrieve the body and set a funeral date. What the hell are we supposed to do?"

"This shit is really fuckin' odd, Paolo. Something is going on with this case. I've never seen a body go missing on any case I've ever worked."

"Christ, what do I tell Abby?"

"Don't fucking know, brother. I'll make a few calls, give them some bullshit line that the funeral home can't pick up the body until the medical board reviews the

autopsy or some shit like that.”

“Okay, I guess. I’ll tell Abby what’s going on.

She’s going to be pissed.”

“Better you than me! What funeral home is she

using?”

“Choy Funeral Home. It’s on the corner of Cherry

and Ninth Street.”

“I have a contact in the fifth district. I’ll call him

and have him pay them a personal visit. Let them know

officially that the autopsy is under investigation for some

procedural bullshit. That should buy me a few days to

figure out this shit.”

“Alright, Richards. Thanks for the heads up. If you

don’t hear from me for a few days, send a car over to see if

Abby beat my ass after telling her the good news.”

"Will do, partner." Richards disconnected the call, put his hands on his hips and hung his head in mock defeat. "Sons-a-bitches always make shit hard."

*****

DeLuca delayed talking with Abby about the missing body of her twin from the morgue, the twin she only learned she had during the fallout from PennVille State Hospital kidnapping. All her life, Abby had felt a part of her was missing. She thought it was about her parents giving her up for adoption, which is why she spent hours web-surfing for clues as to her birth parent's identities and where she could find them. She had fantasies of reuniting with them under the best of circumstances. And living happily ever after. Those fantasies were fueled by many glasses of Yellowtail, her favorite cheap wine, and pictures of happy families reunited by the now popular DNA database websites.

Paolo walked outside into the backyard of Abby's home which she made into a beautiful living area. Paolo called the open-air room the *vaa-ron-dah*, using his best Thurston Howell the Third accent to tease his fiancée. He knew Abby would be lounging there on her favorite overstuffed wicker couch.

She smiled when she saw him approach then resumed reading her book.

"Abby, we need to talk."

"Uh-oh. Is this the you're-a-great-girl-but-I-just-want-to-be-friends speech? Cause if it is, you're too late, buddy. You're not getting out of this alive." When she saw that her attempt at humor didn't change his glum expression, she closed her book, sat upright and patted the chair cushion next to her.

Paolo sat, but he only sat half on the cushion and clasped his hands together with interlaced fingers on his knees.

"This must be serious. What's going on, Paolo. You're scaring me a little bit."

"I'm not really sure what's going on, Abby. I spoke with Richards earlier today. He gave me some news about your sister's body."

"Did he say the funeral home picked it up?"

"Not exactly."

"What exactly did he say?"

Paolo took a breath, "He said the morgue can't find her body."

"What the fuck do you mean, they can't find her body? How the fuck do you lose a body, Paolo? It's not like it could get up and walk away!"

"I-I don't know, Abby. I don't understand it either. Richards is making some calls to figure out what happened."

Tears rolled down Abby's cheeks, and this tugged at Paolo's heart strings, because he was again powerless to help Abby. All he could do was be there for her and hold her . . . if she would let him.

Abby lowered her head and let out a string of words—the same words she had said to Paolo when they first met, the same words she had uttered at him when she hit his pickup truck with her Mercedes sedan. Paolo knew she was extra pissed, because that's when she used those words in that particular order. Paolo knew the lightbulb just illuminated inside Abby's head. "That fucking Taine must have taken her just to screw with us. God! I wish that old fucking bitch was dead!"

"That's what Richards and I think too."

"We need to take a ride to Chinatown and confront that hateful woman." Abby stood from the couch.

"Wait . . . What good—"

"Don't try to stop me, Paolo. I'm going with or without you. She entered the house and slammed her book onto the kitchen table.

"I'll drive!" Paolo said in hopes of calming Abby a bit as he ran after her.

One

Déjà vu

Paolo pulled his blue and rust colored Chevy pick-up truck into the open space across the street from the Hua Grocery store at 934 Race Street. He had a feeling of Déjà vu as it was where he and Brennan first confronted Taine not yet knowing who she was.

"This is just like ground hog day" Paolo said under his breath.

Abby let the comment go without a remark other than a comment on the most mundane thing she could, the name of the grocery store. "Flower, what a stupid name for a grocery store."

"Yeah, it used to be New Lin Grocery, then it was something else like Yong's or Yang's. Taine must change the name of the place every month just to screw with people."

"It's gonna be named burnt up mother fucking building when I get done with her" Abby said in such an irate tone that Paolo had to try to calm her down as she climbed out of his small two door pick up. She was two steps ahead of him and gaining distance as she crossed the street toward the store front. Paolo had to run to catch up with her, he almost vaulted over an oncoming car, two seconds slower and he would have been road kill. He jumped in front of Abby as she was about to enter.

"Abby, I know you're pissed, but let's go in with cooler heads. If Taine is here, her crew will be armed, and I don't have a weapon on me."

She stared at him, realizing the odds of the situation. Abby reached into her oversized hand bag and pulled out the Glock Paolo had given her after the Pennville fiasco. "I've got one" she said brandishing it around like a toy.

Paolo wrestled the weapon away from Abby as she cussed at him. When he turned his back, she beat him with both fists until her anger calmed a bit. "Seriously Paolo, I wasn't going to use it. I just want to scare the bitch, like she does me."

"Taine doesn't know that! Christ Abby, I want us to live through this little shopping spree of ours. Please, I'll keep the weapon, you do the talking."

"I'll keep the weapon," Abby said mocking Paolo as she pulled on the glass door to enter. The door didn't move. It just made a metallic thumping sound as the silver dead bolt bumped against the metal frame. Abby shook the door, rattling it on its hinges as she cussed and screamed Taine's name.

"You better open this fucking door Taine if you know what's good for you." The door rattling continued until Abby tired of the game. She slammed both palms against the lettered glass until her hands hurt from the continued attempts to alert Taine to her presence. She huffed as she turned away from the door, frustrated that she was still standing outside.

"Abby," Paolo said.

"What?" she answered ready to pounce in anger.

"Read the sign."

"What sign?" she asked in return.

"The one that says *ring bell for service.*"

Abby reddened, infuriated that Paolo would point out such a trivial item while he knew she was near the edge of becoming irrational. "Read the sign? I'll show you read the sign you stinking old age home escapee." And with that, Abby picked up the green metal city sanitation trash can and with all of her small stature strength, heaved it at the glass door. When it bounced off the glass, and landed back at her feet, Abby could do nothing but laugh at the outcome.

"Guess I'll try ringing the bell," she said as she moved closer to Paolo and the bell button. "Smart ass," she said as she eyed Paolo while he smirked in her direction.

*****

A young girl in her mid-teens unlocked the door and pushed it open just enough for her to speak to Abby. "We don't open till noon, ma'am."

Abby was taken aback at the young girl indicating that she was old enough to be called ma'am. "Ma'am? I'm not old enough to be called ma'am little girl."

"Whatever!" the girl replied with little interest.

"We're here to see Taine."

"She's not here."

"Sure, she's not. Tell her Abby Woo is here to see her."

"I know who you are. Everyone on Race Street knows who you are, matter of fact, everyone in Chinatown knows who you guys are. And, I was told to tell you, *She's not here.*"

"I want to talk to her. Where is she?" Abby insisted on continuing the conversation.

"Not here," the girl said disinterestedly and started to pull the door closed.

Abby pulled the door full open with both hands and grabbed the teen by the collar of her off-brand button down shirt. She pushed the girl through the door and up against the counter as Paolo lagged behind.

"Where the fuck is she?" Abby asked getting red and angry with the teens lack of interest. The girl with absolutely no fear at this attack, tilted her head to the right

and directed Abby and Paolo to the back room with her
eyes. "See, that wasn't so hard . . . was it?" Abby said as
she straightened the girl's shirt.

"Maybe we shouldn't hurt the little Asian girl while
we're looking for Taine! Okay babe?"

"I got this Paolo."

In the back room, at the same table Taine and Paolo
had tea several months ago, sat a woman who was
obviously waiting for the two of them. "Sit." Was all she
offered.

"Where's Taine?" Abby asked again.

"All in good time Miss Woo."

"I'm not in the mood for games sweetheart. Tell the
queen mother that I am here, waiting to see her."

"Taine is not here." Abby began to protest;
however, the woman interrupted her. "I have been

instructed to give you the location of Taine, but only if you agree to her terms."

"Why does everything have to be an agreement with her. I just want a face-to-face conversation with no negotiations."

"It is a simple request, and will only take up twenty minutes of your time."

"Let me guess," Paolo interjected. *"A cup of tea?"*

"Of course, tea, Mr. DeLuca. Business is always preceded with the formality of tea. Please, both of you, sit. I will guarantee your safety while you are here, even though you attacked my granddaughter for no reason other than to gain entry to my store. I should have called the police."

"Maybe you should teach the bitch some manners and how to respect adults." Abby said with no respect for the woman.

"Mr. DeLuca, please educate your fiancée on the formalities of doing business within a Chinese establishment. I would think, given her heritage; she would know about our customs. But then again, she may be nothing more than the . . ."

"Banana" the teen girl whispered to her grandmother.

"Yes, as my granddaughter has reminded me, *the banana she appears to be.*"

Abby had not heard that remark, or been called that name since grade school. It still bothered her to no end. A minor insult, a micro aggression as they call it today. A name that meant that although she appeared Chinese outside, she was nothing more than a white girl on the inside. Someone with no ties to her heritage, and someone trying to be something she knew nothing about. That remark made Abby remember all of her personal history.

Her abandonment by her birth parents, the adoption by her devout Jewish step-parents, her endless search for something to call her life history, and, of course, the death of a twin sister she never knew she had until the twin was dead at Taine's hands.

The girl that answered the door placed a serving tray on a side table. She set the tea cups and kettle with practiced precision on the table between the three adults. Her grandmother nodded approval as she spoke to Abby, "As I have with Su Anne, perhaps one day you will allow me to instruct you in the ways of our traditions Miss Woo."

"Perhaps. And perhaps you can explain why people like you are so easily led around like sheep by a woman older than dirt."

Tea was served, and when all had consumed it in silence, the woman called grandmother gave an envelope to Abby. "Miss Woo . . . Mr. DeLuca, Taine asked that if you came by, I was to give this envelope to you. She asked that you follow its instructions to the letter. If you do, she will meet you at the place described within. If not, as usual, she will know and you will never find the location of your sisters remains."

Abby was unaware that grandmother knew why they had come today. Paolo was not surprised. "Tell Taine we're coming for the body. If she gives us anything other than Abby's sister's remains, I'm going to kill her. Make no mistake." Paolo said.

Grandmother just nodded her head and stood, indicating the meeting had come to an end. "My granddaughter will show you out." The teen girl held her hand, palm up indicating they should return the way they came.

The girl called Su Anne, unlocked the glass door to allow Abby and Paolo to exit. Paolo pushed the door toward the street and stepped through. He waited for Abby to follow. The young girl spoke to Abby just as she stepped through the door to the sidewalk in a hushed almost secretive tone.

"Taine is planning something for you Miss Woo. Grandmother says we are not to go against anything Taine says, but my grandmother is old and afraid for her life."

"Planned? Like what?" Abby asked as Paolo stood close by.

"Grandmother says that Taine wants you eliminated. You and Mr. DeLuca, and the detective."

"And why are you telling me this? Aren't you afraid for your life, and your grandmother's life?"

"Yes, but I cannot talk now. Grandmother will know I spoke to you if I do not return soon. Here is my number. Call me after midnight tonight when grandmother is in bed."

"I will, Miss . . ."

"I am Kang Su Anne. Please call me Su Anne."

"Su Anne," Abby said. "Paolo and I will call you tonight, after midnight."

"If I answer in Chinese, it is not safe to talk. You must go now; it is not safe for you here." With that, the girl locked the door, turned, and ran to the rear of the store leaving Abby and Paolo standing on the sidewalk somewhat puzzled at what had just transpired.

"What do you think? I mean about the girl?" Abby said.

"Could all be a lie. Lord knows Taine is a master manipulator. Or . . . she's another fly caught in Taine's masterful web doing as Taine told her."

*****

Paolo and Abby sat in the Chevy pick-up and eyed the envelope they were given by the woman called Grandmother. In exquisite calligraphy, Abby's name graced the face of the envelope, and on its reverse, along the sealed flap, her name was printed in Chinese logographs. This appeared to be a formal invitation from Taine, but an invitation to what?

Abby opened the envelope using her manicured nails to separate the flap from its resting place. She pulled the index sized card from within, handing the envelope to Paolo. She read it aloud so Paolo could be included in Taine's instructions.

"Miss Woo, you and your fiancé have become a constant burden, one which I wish to eliminate. I will meet you at the Rising Sun hotel on Delaware Avenue at noon on Friday. There shall be no need for Detective Richards to attend, or for him to concern himself with our gathering. The prize you seek is close by. There are only two instructions for you to follow, arrive at precisely noon, and

do not inform Detective Richards of the meeting. I will, as I

always do, know if you have alerted him to our meeting."

At the bottom of the card, Taine hand signed her name in

Chinese.

Paolo tilted the photo card that was in the envelope

toward Abby, "This must be where we are supposed to

meet her on Friday. I've passed by it several times, thought

it was deserted, It's definitely a shithole."

"Let me see that," Abby said as she pulled the card

from Paolo's hand. She looked at the postcard picture of

the Rising Sun Hotel and commented, "The place is a

dump." Turning the card over, she read the description of

the pictured establishment on the rear of the card. "Historic

my ass!" she said mocking the property. "I was there two

years ago looking for a guy named Pao-Tzu. He was

supposed to have known someone who knew my birth

parents. Shit didn't pan out. Owner said he never heard of

anyone name Pao. Another internet dead end." Abby sighed.

"Probably some shit Taine set up to lead you on another goose chase. Bitch has her hands into everything."

"Yeah, hate that bitch more every day. Especially since Richards found the tracking software on my laptop. It had to be her . . ."

"She does own Computer Logic, and all this shit leads back to them and the damn thumb drive from Franklin Bank."

"What? You still have it?" Abby knew the answer but asked anyway.

"I gave a copy to Taine at Pennville, Richards had a copy, but he sent it to the news agencies, I still have the original from the deposit box. May still do us some good. Maybe."

"Why do you say that?" Abby asked, curious as to what good it could possibly do as all the information on the drive was out.

"There's one file on the drive I didn't make a copy of."

"Why? What the hell could be in the file that we already don't know about?"

"The file is labeled sixth district."

"That's where Richards works out of. Shit! Is he named in the file?" Abby asked afraid of the answer.

"No, but Captain Watts is, and there is an amount of four hundred thousand next to his name."

"Watts is an ass, why did you hold it back? We don't owe him anything."

"Yeah, we don't, but Richards does. I haven't told him yet and I'm not sure I need to or want to."

"Christ! I hate this shit Paolo! Why is she so involved in our lives?"

Paolo thought a moment before rendering a solution, "We need to put an end to her Abby."

"Put an end to her," Abby thought about those words. "You mean kill her? I can't do that Paolo!" Abby said emphatically. "Even after all the shit she's done to me, done to us."

"You can't . . . but I can."

"You made me a fucking promise Paolo. Remember? And after Pennville, you promised me again that there would be no more . . ." She couldn't say the word.

"I did, and I do remember. But we can't let this go on any longer." Paolo argued.

Abby was almost in tears at the thought of another life being taken, even if it was Taine's. "I still have the nightmares Paolo. About all the shit that happened at the

bank, at Pennville, even what happened to Brennan I can't

forget. As much as I hate Taine, I can't justify you killing

her."

"It's the only way Abby." Paolo told her.

"You do this and we're done . . ." Abby said unable

to complete the sentence again

Paolo didn't say a word after Abby's threat. He

knew that if he did what he was planning, Abby would

follow through with her ultimatum. He started the Chevy,

slammed it into gear, and drove off. They rode home in

silence, stayed silent the rest of that day, and didn't speak

again until the call with Su Anne.

Midnight Monday.

Abby woke Paolo who was asleep on the couch. They

hadn't spoken since they left Hua Grocery earlier that day.

Abby nudged him hard, damn near pushing him off the sofa

and told him, "Wake the hell up, it's time to call Su Anne."

He rose begrudgingly, placing his hands on the cushion

beside him as Abby sat next to him. She dialed Su Anne's

number and put the phone on speaker for both of them to

hear. It rang several times, enough to make them wonder if

the girl was going to answer. She finally did.

"Ni hao." a very quiet voice said, almost too quiet

to hear.

"It's Abby."

"Yes," the voice repeated.

Abby was confused at the opening of the

conversation as Paolo spoke up, "Su Anne, Is someone in

the room with you?"

"Yes!" Su Anne repeated.

"Guess you can't talk now, should we call back

later?"

"Yes, talk." The girl said.

"There is someone in the room with her Abby. Probably watching her. Be careful what you say to her." Paolo instructed Abby.

"What did you want to tell us that you couldn't at the store?" Abby began. There was no answer, just muffled sounds coming through the phone, and then . . .

"Wǒ wǎndiǎn zài dǎ gěi nǐ" Su Anne said. (I will call you later.)

"Hello?" Abby said as the phone disconnected. "Shit!" The pair sat there, unmoving and not speaking for the next half hour. Paolo had leaned back and closed his eyes as Abby sat motionless staring at her phone, and touching the dial icon every time the phone was about to go dark. Finally, it rang at 12:35 a.m.

"Hello?" Abby answered hoping it was Su Anne, putting the phone back on speaker.

"Sorry, grandmother woke up when you called. I had to wait until she fell asleep again to call you back."

"Can you tell me what you could not say at the store." Abby instructed the teen.

"Taine wants to eliminate you and Mr. DeLuca, and then the police detective."

"Detective Richard's?" Abby asked.

"Yes, she will send the red headed woman to kill him just like the Marshal from Texas."

"Do you know who she is?" Paolo asked.

"Taine most times calls her Woods, I sometimes hear Taine call her The Hammer, but I am not sure why."

"What about my sister's body, do you know where it is?" Abby asked pushing the conversation along.

"Yes."

"Where is it, Su Anne?" Abby asked with a hard tone.

After a long a long pause, Su Anne spoke. "First you must agree to one thing before I tell you."

"Christ." Abby said. "You're acting just like Taine. What do you want?"

"Protection. You get me out of here before you meet Taine on Friday. The only way she will not find me is if you hide me. Maybe at your house, maybe with the police detective."

"What about your grandmother? Is she in need of help?" Paolo asked.

"She's not really my grandmother, just a name we call her." Su Anne replied.

"Understood." Paolo said.

"How do we know this isn't part of Taine's plan to eliminate us?" Abby asked.

"You will have to trust me, Miss Woo. I mean you no harm." Su Anne said

"Fine." Abby answered back with a noticeable irate tone.

"When you come get me, I will tell you where your sister is. Meet me at the Wearhouse across the street from the Hotel. I will be inside waiting. Come before sunrise on Wednesday."

"I'll be there." Paolo told the girl.

"Come alone. Miss Woo must not be seen near the hotel or the warehouse before Friday." The phone went silent as Abby sat in wonder at the conversation.

"I really don't like this Paolo." Abby said hesitantly in an exaggerated voice.

"If the girl knows where you sister's body is, and I can get her away from Taine on Wednesday, maybe we can find her remains and not have to meet Taine on Friday."

"It's too dangerous. She may have set this whole thing up."

"She probably has." Paolo Said. "Only thing we can do is as Su Anne asked. I'll meet her Wednesday morning. You need to go stay with your parents until Friday. Just to be safe."

"I wouldn't get them involved in this shit Paolo."

"They're already involved Abby. You'll be better off with them until Friday. That way you're not alone."

"Alone. Where will you be?" Abby said.

"With Su Anne until I get her to a safe house. I'll be back by Friday so we can meet Taine. Meanwhile, I'll get a message to Richards telling him to watch out for Woods."

"Taine will know you fucking contacted him Paolo." Abby scolded him.

"Maybe," Paolo shot back, "but it's a chance I have to take."

"I?" Abby said. "What happened to we?"

"What did you tell me in the Chevy outside the store?"

"But --" Abby had no more words as Paolo walked out her front door. She ran after him stopping just inside, calling after him, "Paolo! You can't just leave!"

Two

Friday Morning

Three days had past, since Abby and Paolo spoke a word to each other. As a matter of fact, Paolo hadn't been home. He left Abby's house after the call with Su Anne ended, and hadn't returned since he went to meet her. Abby suffered through a terrible night of sleep, and was out of bed at five a.m. calling Paolo's cell again and again. The phone always went to voice mail with every redial. This time she left a message for him, "Where the fuck are you, Paolo? I know what I said to you, but the truth is, I need you, I'll always need you. I will not live without you. Please call me . . . um . . . it's Friday . . . we need to meet Taine at noon . . . okay?"

Abby, although dead tired and wanting to crawl back into bed to hide from the day, showered, dressed, and attempted to eat. She managed to eat a slice of toast, but threw up from the amount of anxiety she was having. She brushed her teeth, rinsed with mouthwash, and then took double the medication for the anxiety attack she was having. The pills made her even more sluggish than the restless night of sleep. The best word she used to describe herself when she was like this, was numb.

It was 11 a.m. and Paolo still hadn't returned her call. She tried his number once more before heading out to meet Taine at the Rising Sun Hotel. The call, as always, went to voice mail. "Hey, Paolo. It's 11 a.m., time to go, I hope you'll meet me outside the hotel. I need you to be there for me and for Abhijaya. Listen, I drank way too much last night, and I still didn't sleep. I took my anxiety meds this morning . . . and I'm feeling . . . you know . . . numb, I guess. I don't know what's going on with you or where you are. But please, call me, okay? I love you."

Abby disconnected the call as she was rambling and making little sense. She got into the new SUV that she talked Paolo into buying to replace his piece of shit pick-up truck, which he kept anyway. She flung her purse across the front seat, and started the engine. When she looked in the rear-view mirror, she didn't recognize the woman looking back at her. For the first time in years she prayed, "Please God, let me get through this day and bring Abhijaya home . . . and Paolo too."

She pulled the lever into reverse, and backed into the brick pier at the end of her driveway. "Shit! Paolo's gonna kill me for denting his new vehicle." Putting the car in park, Abby cried until her neighbor knocked on the driver's window. She lowered the window, and the neighbor got his first look at Abby.

"My God! You okay Abby? You look like hell."

"No, I'm not okay, but I don't have time to talk. I have a meeting at noon and I gotta go. Can't be even one second late or it's over."

"You sure I can't help?" he asked with genuine concern.

"Yeah, maybe you can. If you see Paolo, tell him I went to the hotel."

"Which hotel?"

"He'll know. Sorry, I really gotta run Noah." She closed the window and pulled forward repositioning the car, and backed out into the street. She sped off, smoking the tires, and leaving her neighbor standing in a cloud of odorous smoke.

*****

Friday Noon.

Abby waited as long as she could outside of the Rising Sun Hotel for Paolo to show up. This was unusual for him; he was never late for anything. He always said that if you're early, you're on time, if you're on time, you're late. It was a military thing, he had told her, something instilled in him in basic training by a drill instructor he credited with turning his life around. It was a quirk of his, never late for anything, even the most mundane of appointments.

Abby took the three wooden steps onto the covered front porch of the hotel. All the signage on the building was faded and hard to read. It was all hand painted and lettered from sometime in the 1930's. The floorboards creaked as she traversed the width of the porch to the front doors. Large black hinges with intricate carved designs accented the oak doors, which in turn held the most ornate etched glass windows Abby had ever seen in any building she had visited in Philadelphia. The scene on the etched windows depicted the early days of Philadelphia's Delaware Avenue. "Beautiful!" Abby thought as she was distracted for mere seconds from her mission here at noon.

"Exactly noon," Abby announced as she walked through the double doors and into an antiquated lobby as the chimes of the grandfather clock rang out in agreement. The man behind the desk was dressed in era appropriate garb as he signaled for her to approach the counter.

"Welcome Miss Woo," He began as he spun a large ledger book resting on an antique turn table to face her. "Please sign the guest registry."

"I'm not checking in, I'm here to meet Taine." Abby told the old man.

"Yes, this is a mere formality; however, all of our visitors are required to sign our registry as it is an important historical record of who has visited our establishment." Abby picked up the quill and dipped it into the inkwell and signed her formal name. She scanned the left page as she wrote and then the right when finished. Paolo's name was eight spaces above hers under the heading Wednesday, 7

May 2020. She put the quill down and looked at the old man, "May I?" She asked, indicating she wanted to flip through the pages of the ledger. She scanned several pages noting the prominent names that graced the pages of the ornate ledger book. Paolo's name also appeared under Tuesday's heading. Captain Watts name was several lines above Paolo's, along with others she knew from hearing Richards talk about his fellow workers at the sixth district.

"What the fuck were you doing here on Tuesday Paolo? Maybe meeting Watts?" she said aloud as someone behind her called her name.

"Miss Woo, please come this way." Called a woman in a maid's uniform. The woman led Abby to the dining room and asked her to sit at the end furthest from the door marked *kitchen staff only*. Abby did as she was asked, placed her opened purse just in reach of her right hand and gazed at the butt of the Sig Sauer hidden within. She looked around the room, taking in all possible exits as Paolo had taught her to do. There were only two, the open double door she had just walked through, and the entrance to the kitchen, which probably led to a back alley or loading area behind the hotel.

She looked at the black and white framed photos gracing the walls and glared at one in particular. Curiosity over took her and she rose and walked over to the faded pale blue papered wall. In a picture labeled *The Architect,* stood a woman in a driver's uniform next to a well-dressed man wearing a three-piece suit, a Fredrick Fedora hat, and round framed eye glasses. The room she was standing in was the same room in the photo. A chill came over Abby as she inched closer to the photo and realized the girl in the driver's uniform, the young girl in the photo, was Taine. The photo was hand dated 1936. A voice from behind her said, "The man in the photo is Huan-Yue, he was known as *The Architect.* He was another verbally abusive man who helped shape my young life, and one of the first men I killed to take control of the triad here in Philadelphia. I was barely seventeen years old in that photograph.

Abby spun round, realizing that Taine had walked in the room and she had never heard a sound of the old woman approaching. She also realized that her purse was on the table, too far for her to reach if Taine tried anything. Abby spoke to calm herself, "If you were seventeen in this photo, that would make you about 100 years old Taine, surprised you can still get around under your own power."

"Give or take some years. Life has been good to me Miss Woo. Fortunately, my lineage offers a long life for the women of my family tree. My mother and grandmother each lived to the age of one hundred and ten years, although I did not see them after I left Hong Kong, I was able to follow their lives remotely, thanks to an acquaintance who still goes between Hong Kong and America. And as you have said Miss Woo, I am too stubborn to die." Taine said as she walked at a snail's pace to the chair with its back to the kitchen door. The maid pulled the chair out for Taine to sit in, and Taine grabbed her hand to aide in sitting in the chair.

"Seems you're not getting along so well Taine. Maybe the next time we meet, I'll bring along a walker, the kind with the tennis balls on the legs . . ." Abby jested, trying to insult Taine.

"Ahhh, an attempt at humor Miss Woo. I have been insulted and humiliated many times in my life. Your's pale by comparison, unlike your Mr. DeLuca who threatens to kill me along with his insult."

"Paolo was here, I saw his name in your ledger, along with Captain Watts, and Officer Harding. Two more of your paid for policemen I assume."

"Harding was into horse racing, he bet far above his meager policeman's wages, he could not pass a betting house without wagering. Soon he was in too deep to get out, now, when I need a favor, he provides it."

"And Watts" Abby asked hoping Taine would fill her in on more of the sixth district crew.

"Yes, Captain Watts, such a sad tale. His wife and daughter were injured in a motorcar accident. One you can say I had a hand in. Before they died from their injuries, the hospital bills amounted to over four hundred thousand dollars. An anonymous benefactor satisfied the demand for payment from his creditors." Taine Confessed.

"You set him up, had a hand in the death of his wife and daughter."

"I needed an inside man in the sixth district, one with position and power to do as I wanted. He had a choice, accept the payout from the benefactor, or lose all that he had left of his family. I have ties to the family court, his son was only four at the time of his wife's death, and the boy would have been taken from him if he didn't agree to my terms."

"God, you are a heartless monster Taine. How can you play on people's emotions without an ounce of guilt? Doesn't this bother you at all, the way you manipulate and use everyone?" Abby asked with a new level of disgust with Taine.

"I learned many years ago who I truly am. If you need to lay blame for all I have done, you must blame Chang Lo. I am sure Marshal Brennan informed you of her conversation at the prison with him, before her untimely demise."

"You fucking killed her too . . ." Abby said, informing Taine of what she already knew.

"I eliminated a loose end, Miss Woo. I have a very loyal assassin who, because of a man, will kill for the pleasure of killing. Miss Woods is highly skilled. As your detective friend Richards will soon find out." Taine admitted.

"Why Richards? He didn't do anything to you that you had not earned."

"Retribution Miss Woo. Miss Brennan was the first to die because she was a friend of your fiancé. Richards will be dead before the night is out, again because of his friendship with your future husband. Then just Mr. DeLuca and you remain. As for your surrogate parents, I've yet to decide."

"Why? Why them? Is it because we took down your empire? Put an end to your crime syndicate?" Abby said."

"You did not end anything Miss Woo, you merely delayed what I had planned. Now that you have some answers, may we get down to business?" Taine asked somewhat perturbed. The old woman banged her cane on the floor twice and the kitchen staff brough out tea. Taine did all of her business over tea. It added a bit of civility to an otherwise one-sided agreement.

"What do you want from me Taine? We don't need all the melodrama to discuss business, as you call it."

"Tea just makes what I am about to tell you more pleasant Miss Woo. I have this blend brought in from Chang Lo's homestead in Hong Kong, another property that was once his which is now mine. I do allow him some of each yearly crop while he is in prison. It reminds him of who is in charge, and it humiliates him at the same time. That is, until he died of extreme old age in his prison cell." Taine almost smiled.

"All the horrible things you say he did to you, and he's the one man you never killed."

"What I did to him was much worse than death. His fate was to remain alive and to think of all he had done to me, and to Maylin. He had a lifetime to relive all of the decisions he made, and to suffer for them."

"Who's Maylin?" Abby asked since this was the first time she had heard the name.

"Perhaps another time . . ."

"She was a friend." Abby said matter-of-factly.

Taine sighed. "My only true friend at the House of Lo. He killed her when I would not make myself available to him sexually. The man, like most men, was a pig. Only caring for his own needs."

"I'm sorry you lost your friend, Taine." Abby confessed.

Taine was in deep thought of the memory when Abby spoke to her. "Again, what do you want from me."

Taine finished her tea, and the maid poured each of them another serving. "It is not what I want from you Miss Woo. It is what you want from me."

"Such as?"

"The location of your sister's remains, and," Taine paused with a sip of tea, which seemed to drag on for hours. "And unfortunately for you, the location of Mr. DeLuca."

Abby teared up a bit before finding the ability to speak. "You have Paolo? so help me if you hurt him, I will kill you myself Taine."

"Mr. DeLuca attempted to take my property from me. Miss Woods foiled his attempt. He is soft hearted, and therefore easy to manipulate, always wanting to save the day . . . to be the hero, like the knight in your fairy tales."

"Take your property? What did he try to take?" Abby asked.

"Not what Miss Woo, who!" Taine corrected her.

"Fuck! Su Anne! That lying little bitch. I told him something was wrong with her story."

"Do not blame the child Miss Woo. She was just a pawn, and like you, she had no choice in what she needed to do." Taine told Abby.

"Is Paolo alive?"

"For now."

Abby placed her hand on her purse, thinking about putting an end to Taine once and for all. She placed her hand on the butt of the Sig Sauer, lost in thought for mere moments about her conversation with Paolo while in his Chevy."

"If you kill me now Miss Woo. Mr. DeLuca and Miss Abhijaya will both be dead before the day is at an end."

Abby froze in mid movement at what she thought she just heard. Paolo she already knew was still alive, but her sister, Abhijaya . . . ALIVE. . . it can't be true. She was pronounced dead at Pennville.

"Abhijaya's alive?" Abby asked in surprise.

"Perhaps, perhaps not." Taine said, "But if you agree to do as I ask, and fulfill our contract, it will be the only way for you to know for sure."

"If I do what you want, I get both Paolo and Abhijaya . . ." Abby said as a fact.

"Time will tell." Taine retorted. Taine tilted her head and the maid who Abby realized had been in the room the entire time, handed Abby a video pad. "Press play, Miss Woo."

Abby hit the play icon and a video, complete with sound and theatrical lighting, streamed across the screen. The video began outside the hotel, meandered across the road and showed the entrance to the building across the street from the building she was now in. Two men were beating Paolo who was bound and gagged. He was on his knees, hands tied behind his back to his ankles. When the beating stopped, Paolo fell face first into the cement floor of the warehouse just across the street. The camera moved in close to his face, and a voice told him to speak to prove he was still alive.

"Fuck you . . ." was all he was able to say before he fell unconscious.

Abby was angry, so much so that she threw the video pad at Taine. As old as the woman was, her reflexes were those of a woman one quarter her age. Taine blocked the video pad from hitting her head just as the maid slapped Abby with all of the strength she had. Abby fell to the carpeted wooden floor. She stood, wiping a trickle of blood from her mouth.

"What the fuck do you want me to do Taine."

"Just one simple task. One that will prove not too difficult given your current state of mind." Taine said softly.

"Will you fucking tell me for God's sake."

"There is a file being held in the property room at the sixth district police station. I want you to retrieve it and bring it to me at the warehouse across the street. When you do, I will return Mr. DeLuca to you."

"And Abhijaya?"

"One reward at a time, Miss Woo." Time passed as Abby stood thinking of any possible way to avoid doing as Taine asked. Nothing came to mind.

"I'll do what you want. But I want an answer first." Abby said.

"Yes?" Taine inquired.

"Is Abhijaya alive."

Taine actually smiled at Abby's question, "You are an intelligent woman, Miss Woo. What does your intuition tell you?"

Abby knew that conversation was now pointless, Taine would not elaborate on her sister's fate, no matter how many ways she asked the same question. Taine had her where she wanted her. She gathered her purse, and what was left of her dignity, and headed for the door to the hallway. Just as she turned the knob to open the door to the outside world, Taine strode into the hallway.

"One more thing Miss Woo."

"What now?" Abby said in anger.

"There must be no witness to you taking the file."

"How am I supposed to get in and out of a police district building full of cops without being seen?"

Taine turned her back on Abby and walked toward the kitchen door. "I am sure your Mr. DeLuca has taught you something in your time together Miss Woo. I will see you at the warehouse Sunday evening."

The two women left the building in opposite directions. Abby stared at the warehouse across Delaware Avenue. She knew Paolo was no longer there. They probably move him while Taine laid out the details of her contract with Abby. She pulled out her cell phone and scrolled through the contacts list looking for Detective Richards number. She was just about to press the dial icon when someone spoke from behind her.

"I would not make that call if I were you, Abby." The unknown female voice said to her.

Startled, Abby turned toward the voice and found a remarkably beautiful redhead standing just behind her. She was just a bit shorter than Abby, thin, fair complexion, with seven freckles on her left cheek that resembled the big dipper.

"Miss Woods, or should I call you the Hammer?"

"Whichever you wish, Miss Woo, just don't call Detective Richards, or I'll kill you right here."

Abby put her phone back into her purse, shouldered the bag and turned toward her vehicle. She looked back at the woman named Woods, wanting to say something. But Woods spoke first.

"Have a pleasant day, Miss Woo. I will be watching you." She turned and went back inside the hotel.

Three

Wednesday

Paolo arrived at the Delaware Avenue warehouse at four a.m. He had been here before, but only outside the front entrance. He had done some odd jobs in the Penn's Landing area, some auto mechanic work, some carpentry for a friend opening a store at the strip mall just up the street, and some surveillance work when he was looking for a flop house, the place he stayed was just down the street from the warehouse. He wondered if Pitt was still hanging around the motel, offering his services to anyone who needed something done for a double sawbuck buck. He smiled at the memory of the conversation he and Pitt had the night before he set out for Pennville to rescue Abby from Taine.

Paolo leaned back in the seat of his piece of crap Chevy pick-up after setting the alarm on his watch to five a.m. His training in Spec Ops never really left him, he was just a bit rusty, although he used it more since all this started with the Franklin Bank robbery, Abby's kidnapping, and the Pennville fiasco. He used a lot of fire power there, more than he wanted to. Most of his cache of weapons was gone, confiscated by the ATF after Pennville, his two Sea-Box containers containing all of his comm and computer gear were destroyed in the explosion that rocked the old Navy Yard property, plus, his Ninja motorcycle was at the bottom of the Delaware after a drunken escapade the weekend after Abby was home safe and away from Taine.

The watch alarm chimed twice, and Paolo got out of the pick-up and dropped the key on the floor board. It was a habit; he knew he could always find the key where he left it. The Chevy was such a piece of shit, no one wanted to steal it, even for scrap value. Not much money in rust and Bondo these days. He pulled his wool cap down over his ears as low as it would go, checked the magazines in his twin Beretta 92's, and then slung his tactical sling back pack over his head. He had six extra M9 magazines inside and two smoke grenades, just in case things got out of hand. He smiled at the memory of the conversation he and Brennan had had about all the weapons he had on hand.

Paolo walked casually across Delaware Avenue toward the front of the warehouse. The faded sign on the tall wooden doors read *ZAI-SHUO IMPORTS.* It was obvious to Paolo that this was another of Taine's many property holdings. He tried the door, locked as he suspected, but worth a shot. He followed a worn path to the right side of the warehouse, climbed the half-fallen chain link fence which rattled and clamored under his weight as he traversed it. He put his back to the cold cinder block wall hiding from any eyes alerted by the noise. Just past a flight of metal steps to a second story entry, was a man door, he chose it as his entry point. Paolo scurried along the wall past the stairs and into the shadows of the metal stairway. He looked around and reassured himself that no one was watching him. Paolo looked at the door and pulled on the old rusted padlock, it was solid, as was the chain around the handle and fence post charged to keep it shut. "Shit, need another way in."

Paolo looked down the building toward the dock and the water, nothing. His only possible way in now was at the top of the stairs. Ascending the steps at a pace not to make a sound, Paolo was rewarded with an open door. He put his back to the wall at the top of the stairs, he was now facing the street he came from, and could see the empty steps leading back to the shadows below. Pulling the door slowly with the palm of his right hand, he heard the hinges sing a loud melody of metal-on-metal tunes. Paolo froze, the door and the sound stopped, he gauged the size of the opening but it was still not enough for him to get inside.

Paolo took a breath, grabbed the door knob with his left hand, and the side of the door with his right and lifted the door. To his surprise, the wooden door rose off of its hinges. He stepped inside carrying the door just a few feet into the room and laid the door against an empty wall of shelves. As he scanned the room, he called out, "Su Anne!" It was just loud enough for someone in the room to hear, if that someone was indeed in the room. Nothing.

Paolo opened the next door, it led to a wide mezzanine that ran the perimeter of the warehouse. Office doors dotted the upper level of the warehouse, he didn't have time to check them all for Su Anne, he had to chance it, call out to see if she were here, maybe close by.

"Su Anne!" He said softly, but his voice echoed louder around the large vacant room. "Shit," he muttered, afraid he would be noticed. Seconds later a female voice returned his query.

"Down here . . . under the steps. Follow the catwalk to the steps, I'll be waiting at the bottom."

The hairs on Paolo's neck stood up. He had that feeling again, the one where he advised himself to use better judgement. Cautiously, he traveled the distance to the stairs, and started down.

"Where are you?" He asked again.

"Here . . ." the voice called out.

When Paolo's left foot touched the fourth step from the floor, someone's hands grabbed his ankle and pulled him off his footing. He fell hard, slamming his chest into the edge of the wooden steps, and he felt a rib crack. He slid the remaining steps to the floor, and hit his head on the concrete. Dazed, Paolo's reaction time was slowed enough to not be able to dodge the kick in the gut. He gasped as he grabbed his gut to protect it from another attack; however, he caught a glimpse of a redheaded woman reaching out toward him.

"Say goodnight Mr. DeLuca!" and with the formality of meeting each other over, Woods jabbed him in his exposed neck with a syringe, she injected the etorphine into his bloodstream. Paolo tried to fight the drug, but he was incapacitated enough that Woods could easily handcuff him. He lost the battle almost as soon as it begun.

Four

Su Anne

The young girl sat terrified in the rear seat of the pearl-colored Escalade next to a semi-unconscious DeLuca. Her tears stained her ghostly complexion as she feared Taine's retribution. Grandmother either overheard her conversation with Abby and Paolo, or Taine had bugged her phone and learned of her plan to run from the triad's protection. Either way, she was deep in the thick of things.

Woods gazed at her in the rear-view mirror and stoked her fear, "You fucked up big time little one. Taine is furious with you and your plan to leave the nest. She left it up to me as what happens to you." Woods had a slight smile on her face as she watched the girl shiver at her threat.

Woods slowed to make the right turn onto East Oregon Avenue, before she accelerated, Su Anne attempted to open the rear door and jump from the slow-moving vehicle. In frustration, she pulled on the handle repeatedly until she knew the escape attempt was fruitless. Woods laughed out loud and spoke to Su Anne like a mother disciplining her child.

"Guess you ever heard of *child proof door locks* little one. Try that again and I'll come back there and beat your boney ass . . .

Su Anne found her voice, even though it was a bit timid, "You're such a bitch!" She folded her arms in defeat, and pouted out her lower lip, as she leaned her head onto the shoulder of her seat mate. One tear tracked down her left cheek, fell, and landed in the open palm of DeLuca. He awoke with a freakishly startling jump, Woods commented, "Welcome back Mr. DeLuca. I was hoping you'd be out until we got to Pennville, but . . . at least you two can get to know each other a little better along the way. Hey . . . I got an idea! Su Anne! Tell DeLuca how fucked up you crack whoring mother is. It's always a good conversation starter." Woods snickered.

Su Anne buried her head into Paolo's chest, trying to hide from Woods verbal assault. Paolo lifted both of his handcuffed wrists and cradled the girls head in a moment of compassion. He spoke so only the girl could hear, "Don't feed her ability to degrade you. You're better than she is." The effects of the drug lingered; however, they were wearing off faster than Woods realized.

At the next intersection, as the Escalade slowed at the traffic light, Paolo shifted his head to the right, silently telling Su Anne to move away from him. Her face indicated that she understood and she moved toward the passenger window. As soon as the vehicle stopped, Paolo reached his cuffed wrists over the driver's seat and wrapped them around the neck of Woods. He pulled with all the strength he could muster. Woods chocked as her eyes grew in response to the attack. She hit the accelerator and then the break in rapid succession causing Paolo to loosen his grip enough for her to reach the pistol on the passenger seat of the SUV. She fired it into the rear seat clumsily several times hitting Su Anne in the forearm and DeLuca in the right shoulder twice. He lost control of his attack and Woods slammed the vehicle into park in the middle of the road. She forced his cuffed arms over her head, threw open the door, jumped out of the SUV and pulled the passenger door open. Woods grabbed a fist full of DeLuca's hair, pulled him from the vehicle, and proceeded to beat him in the head until he had no fight left in him. She managed to get him back into the vehicle, and this time, re-cuffed his hands behind his back. He laid on top of Su Anne, both of them now with injuries from gun shots, and bleeding onto the pearl white seats of the SUV. Su Anne's injuries were superficial, and she had the presence of mind to wrap her jacket arm around the wound to stem the flow of blood. Paolo's however, were server. Woods yelled at Su Anne,

"Put some pressure on his wound so he doesn't fucking die before I can kill him."

Somewhat confused, Su Anne did as she was told. Paolo was bleeding from the front and back of his upper body. Both bullets went through him missing any important organs. She took his shirt off of him and tied it around the wounds as best she could at the behest of Woods.

"It's still bleeding! Su Anne said in a frantic voice.

"You need to make it tighter. Take his belt off and loop it over his shoulder and then under his arm. Pull it as tight as you can." Woods directed the girl through the application of a make-shift tourniquet. Su Anne looped the belt through the buckle and pulled with all of her strength. She managed to get the prong through one of the holes in the black leather, which held everything together, including Paolo. The blood flow slowed, but if they didn't get him to a doctor soon, he would die from the loss of blood.

By this time, the pair were cover in blood and the odor of copper infiltrated Su Anne's nose as a bitter taste sat upon her tongue. This was her first foray into the Taine's brutal world of retaliation at the hands of one of her trusted minions. A woman who, like Taine, held no compassion for anyone other than themselves. Su Anne feared for her life now that DeLuca could no longer help her escape from the world that had become her daily life. She wondered what fate awaited her and her companion once they reached Pennville, wondered if Taine would be there to oversee their demise, or if Woods alone would decide their final fate. All of this reality was playing games with the fragile mind of this sixteen-year-old runaway. A girl caught in the maze of Taine's underworld, a place she could see no escape from. Would Taine or Woods kill her she thought again, or would they put her into a life of prostitution, there are many men in Philadelphia that would pay to be with an Asian girl of her age. Or, would she become what her mother was, a drug running pawn in

Taine's chess game, or maybe they just put her out of her

misery and allow her to die and not suffer from their life

choices for her.

*****

The Escalade pulled through the double wide chain

link gates at the former State Hospital. As soon as it was

through, the man posing as a ground's keeper, closed the

gate behind it. Pennville was now a tourist attraction for the

morbidly curious, and in the month of October, it was a

state of the art all out Halloween fright fest attraction.

Blood and gore emanated from every building that had

been renovated for the purpose of the side business. This

illusion of an actual business enterprise covered up the real

goings on at Pennville. It was Taine's lair, her place to hide

away many of her subordinates, her guns and ammo cache,

and above all, the perfect opportunity to launder her illegal

income.

Woods pulled up to the front of the main building, the same one where Paolo had found Abby not too many months removed from today. She exited the vehicle, pulled Paolo from the rear seat and ordered Su Anne to come around and help him. A man standing out of sight, just behind the main doors came out and assisted the girl with Paolo. Woods told him to get the herbalist and to have him attend to the girl and DeLuca. She put the pair into the first room she came to, forced Paolo to the black and white tile floor with a slight kick behind the knee. Su Anne looked at her with dagger eyes,

"You didn't need to do that; he can barely stand anyway."

"Sit your ass down next to him and shut the hell up. I've had enough of your shit for one day." Wood spouted.

As soon as Woods left the room, Su Anne knelt close to Paolo and whispered into his ear, "I know I'm being selfish here DeLuca, but you need to get me the hell out of here as soon as you can. Do you hear me DeLuca?" Paolo moaned something that Su Anne took as an affirmation of her request.

The antique office door creaked open and two men walked in, both holding black bags that looked like something out of a 1960's tv medical show. The elder man, who Su Anne recognized as the herbalist from a shop on Race Street, knelt at DeLuca's side. In Chinese he ordered his assistant to remove DeLuca's tourniquet and his blood-soaked shirt. He surveyed the damage from the bullets, and asked his assistant for an antiseptic which he flushed the wounds with. He applied an odorous salve which he covered with something that resembled a banana leaf. Finally, he covered all of the dressings with a wide bandage, and a generous amount of medical grade tape.

"Keep the wounds clean Paako, replace his bandages before sundown, and again in the morning. I will return at noon tomorrow for a follow up."

"Shi!" Paako said to the man in the lab coat.

"I will be at the apothecary If he takes a turn for the worse. Taine has instructed that he must kept alive. He is in your charge Paako, see that no further harm comes to him or there will be repercussions."

"Shi!"

The doctor turned to head out of the room as he spoke, "And tend to the girl, Taine wants to see her as soon as her wounds are cared for."

"I will take a special interest in the young woman Zaho!"

The man in the lab coat turned back toward Paako, walked to within inches of the man and spoke loud enough for Su Anne to hear, "If you touch her in any way other

than to bandage her wounds, I will kill you myself Paako.
Do you understand?"

"I will do as you say . . . for now Zaho, but in the
end, I will get what I want." Paako said as he stared at Su
Anne. She felt repulsed and sickened at the thought of the
man, she needed to get herself out of this situation as it
seemed DeLuca couldn't help himself, let alone her. As
Paako dressed her wounds, she leaned away from him,
attempting to put as much distance between them as
possible.

As he cared for her, he ran his palm up and down
the bare flesh of her arm with slow and tender pressure. Su
Anne felt something come over her, a reaction she had
never experienced before. Her pale skin flushed pink as she
took in a soft breath and a warm feeling involuntarily
overtook her body, he spoke only a few words as her skin
turned to gooseflesh, "Soon you will be mine little one."
The image of this disgusting man doing with her as he

pleased frightened Su Anne to the point of sickness. She leaned toward him and vomited onto the man as he knelt beside her. Women always angered him with little cause, and this violation of his tenderness caused him to strike out at the young girl. He back handed her across her right cheek as she wiped her mouth with the back of her hand. Her eyes rolled toward the ceiling as she fell to the floor unconscious, hitting her head hard on the old marble tile floor.

Taine happened to walk into the room just as the slap was unfolding, she hadn't seen anything prior to Paako striking her prisoner. Woods trailed seconds behind her, when she saw Su Anne out cold on the floor, she knew what Taine's reaction would be.

"Were you not instructed to care for the girl by Zaho?" Taine asked already knowing that he was. The aged woman turned her right palm toward the ceiling just below shoulder height. Woods knew what she wanted without being asked. She pulled her Glock from the holster that rested between her left forearm and her waist. She placed it in Taine's hand and held it by the barrel as the old woman grabbed the grip and slid her forefinger through the trigger guard.

"Look how she has disgraced me," Paako said as he gestured with both hands toward the vomit in his lap.

Taine placed the muzzle of the 9mm pistol to the man's forehead as he remained kneeling. "I asked that she not be harmed. Woods actions, although disappointing, are understandable, yours however, Mr. Paako, were avoidable." Paako never heard the end of the sentence. Taine handed the weapon back to Woods the same way it was given to her. She spoke to Woods as the woman took back her pistol. "Will I need to remind you again that I wish no harm come to Su Anne, or do I need to eliminate the possibility of you not keeping her safe Silvia?"

Woods knew her time was close to being at an end. Taine had only called her by her given name once before this, and that was when she was first recruited.

"No. I will keep her with me at all times to insure nothing else happens to her."

"And Mr. DeLuca?"

"Yes, as well as DeLuca," Woods verbally agreed.

Taine turned and looked Woods directly in the eye, "Do not disappoint me again Miss Woods."

"Understood" was all the woman could say in response to the threat on her life. She gazed at the unconscious pair as she called for assistance. When the men arrived, Woods told them to move the pair to the basement room, the same room that Paolo had found Abby in when Taine had held her hostage after the Franklin Bank robbery.

"Once they are down there, I want you to set up two cots for them, pillows, blankets, bottled water, snacks. We're apparently going into the daycare business and I'm the head babysitter."

The men looked at her as if she were from Venus, but they did exactly as they were told.

"Tell Yang I'll need a table, chair, and a laptop set up down there also." One of the crew ran off to get all that Woods requested. He feared Taine, but he feared Woods just as much. He knew this woman's history, clear back to how she murdered her abusive boyfriend. Each of them knew her nickname was *The Hammer,* and none of them wanted to experience her wrath.

Five

Friday

Abby drove the damaged SUV back to her house just on the outskirts of Philadelphia proper. The entire drive she was thinking of how the hell she was going to get into the sixth district police building, let alone its property room to get the thumb drive that Taine wanted. It was already Friday afternoon, which gave her the rest of the day, and Saturday to complete her unwanted assigned mission. "But how?" she spoke aloud to herself still sitting in the car in her driveway. "What would Paolo do?" she continued.

As she exited the vehicle, a thought flashed across her mind. The corner of her mouth peeked upward as it always did when an idea came to her. She almost ran to the computer in her study, tossing her purse onto the floor of the entryway as the door banged hard behind her.

Slamming her fingers across the keyboard, the screen lit up fully with the entry of her password, *whoami24abby?*

Her password revealed much of her struggles surrounding her life, but now was not the time for her to do her usual internet DNA-N-Me web-based searches. She had more important things to accomplish today. She keyed in the phrase, *recruits,* and, *Philadelphia Police.*

Instantly thousands of Google results appeared, she clicked on the word *image* just under the search bar and photos galore appeared. Several minutes of searching gave her what she wanted, the beginnings of an idea of what she was looking for, the required uniform of an official Philadelphia Police recruit. Khaki pants, black three button cut away collar shirt, black shoes, white name plate with black block lettering, black baseball cap, and the academy patch worn on the left shoulder. Abby made a list of all of the items needed and headed out to the SUV.

Retrieving her purse from the floor where she had left it, she headed into the city for an afternoon of thrift store shopping. She found the shoes at one store, a shirt and pants at another, a name plate with Johnson at a third, and an official looking police ball cap, and a patch two stops later at a place called *All Things Philadelphia,* which was nothing more than a permeant indoor yard sale. As she purchased the last item, she small talked with the owner about the items.

"Did you find everything you were looking for?"

"Sort of. You wouldn't happen to have a police badge by chance?"

The shop owner reached under his counter and pulled out a wooden keepsake box. "I have some replica badges from when I was a collector of all things law enforcement."

He moved some things around in the box and said, "Ah, here she is. An official replica of a Philadelphia policeman's badge."

"Cool!" Abby said trying to sound excited. "How much?"

"Twenty bucks okay?"

"Twenty it is," Abby said as she handed him the cash.

With all of the required items now in her possession, Abby headed home. She walked in the door and went straight to her bedroom. Dropping everything on the bed, she disrobed and tried on all of the clothes. The pants were a tad too tight, but it would be a help she thought as if they were looking at her figure, they wouldn't be scrutinizing her uniform. Out of habit she took a selfie with her phone and damn near posted in on social media. Satisfied that she could pass momentary muster, she changed and began her research on the sixth district headquarters building, its surrounding streets and alleys, its entrance and exit points, and as Paolo taught her, where to park her escape vehicle in a city full of one-way streets. Satisfied that she had all that she needed; it was now a waiting game. It was too late in the day to go on an adventure of infiltration into a building she had never been in, so she thought the next best thing was to do a drive by.

As Abby drove to the Chinatown district, she realized that Paolo had over time, since they had become serious, taught her many survival skills without being so obvious about the teaching. Conversations were something like, "You're parking here"

"Yeah, why?"

"It's better to park one street over, that way your vehicle is already heading in the direction you need to drive when you get in it."

"I don't see what difference it makes."

"Twenty to thirty seconds difference, could be life or death in a bad situation" Paolo said not making Abby feel bad or worry. "Just something to keep in the back of your mind . . . for the future. You know, just in case."

Abby drove around the block several times in opposite directions trying to reconnoiter the area. At one point she parked the car and sat on the bench across the street from the station house, pretending to chat on her cell. She got up, crossed the street, still fake chatting as she stood next to one of the patrol cars parked in the lot beside the building. It was a small building, just a few stories tall with little parking for the official vehicles. A small side alley led to a side door on the building. If she backed up a few steps she could read the sign on the door, it read employees only. A possible exit she thought. Abby strolled to the corner and took several photos of the building from different angles, all to help finalize her entry into an unknown world.

Finally, Abby got back into her SUV and went home. She downloaded all of the pictures from her phone to her multi-screen laptop. Paolo had set up this unit, now she understood why. Multiple screens, multiple images on display and one screen using tabs of googled information.

"The man knows his investigative shit!" Abby said to the monitor in front of her. She did a deep dive into a site she found that provided her with badge numbers and districts. She also googled Watts and Harding. Both names came up in several searches, some with awards and commendations and just as many with derogatory marks against each of the pair.

"Watts," she began, "I can see your reason for taking Taine's offer, although I don't agree. You, Harding, on the other hand, I will bet are the dirty cop other dirty

cops hate."

Abby finished her conversation with herself and the

laptop. She deleted her search history, as Paolo instructed

her to do after each search, and shut the system down.

Folding down the top to the keyboard, Abby placed both

hands on the surface of the computer and prayed for the

second time in several months. It was becoming a habit for

her; one her parents would approve of. Now it was time to

wait, wait until Saturday morning to infiltrate the sixth

district police station building. To wait to get herself into a

situation she had never been in before, she would become a

thief, stealing from the police, right out from under their

collective noses. The thought scared her, but the thought of

losing Paolo overtook her fear.

Six

Saturday

Abby woke early, not that she had slept. She ran over the details of her plan in her head as she prepared for the day. She showered, brushed her teeth, dried her hair and put in into a braided pony tail. She dressed in the mock police cadet uniform, put on the uncomfortable black dress shoes, and the donned the ball cap, tucking the braid through the hole in its rear where the size adjustment elastic band was. Gazing at herself in the full-length dressing mirror in her bedroom, she moved left, then right, each time gauging her appearance. She shrugged her shoulders and tilted her head to once side in skeptic satisfaction. Lastly, she spun far enough around and looked at herself from the back.

"Errrruuggg. Not very flattering." Abby said as she focused on the reflection of her butt in the mirror. Abby checked her minimal make up one last time, went to grab her wallet, and then thought better of it.

"I'll leave this all here, don't want to make some stupid mistake" she thought.

Abby got into Paolo's ratty old jeep, and as bad as it was, it was ten times better than his piece of shit pick-up truck. She couldn't drive her red Mercedes sedan to the district building, she was supposed to be a struggling recruit, not a rich girl trying to impress someone, nor was she supposed to stand out among the crowd. This old red and primer gray Jeep Wrangler was the perfect camouflage along with her thrift store recruit uniform.

Abby took all of the back streets to her destination. The rag top of the Jeep fluttered in the wind as she drove the speed limit, and the plastic fold down combination door and window bounced against the inside of the passenger compartment, making a sound that was reminiscent of a baseball card in a bicycle spoke. By the time she arrived at the sixth district, her hearing was a bit off from all the noise.

As she got out of the jeep, Abby uttered a few derogatory syllables at the vehicle. She finished with, "What a piece of crap."

*****

Abby took the steps to the front door two at a time. The officer coming out held the door as she went in. "Thank you!" she said with a polite smile as she strode past him, and as he stopped walking and checked her out. She walked to the window and knocked, the desk sergeant came around and asked what she wanted.

"Cadet Johnson sir, here to pick up some evidence for Captain Rickenbacker."

"Rickenbacker? I thought that old son of a bitch was dead?"

Abby had to think on her feet, she didn't expect to converse with anyone. "Alive and well and ornery as ever Sargent."

The sergeant looked at her, scrutinizing her a little longer than she was comfortable with. Finally, he spoke, "Take the stairs to the left to the basement. Tell Officer Patterson what you need."

"Thanks!" Abby said as she headed to the basement.

"Recruit!" the desk sergeant yelled as Abby stopped dead in her tracks fearing that she'd been found out.

"Yes sir?"

"Tell that friggin Rickenbacker I said it's time for him to retire."

Relieved, Abby said, "Will do!" She trotted down the steps to the basement property room ready for her next challenge. At the bottom of the steps, the hallway did a U-turn and a long line of blue and white doors all with heavy silver lever handles. Each door had an 8 x 11 plexiglass panel attached at eye level. The paper under the plexiglass announced what each room contained. She worked her way down the hall, passing the silver elevator door, until there were only two left. The one on the right read *Weapons Storage,* and the one on the left read *Evidence Storage.*

"Gotta be it" Abby hoped.

She knocked on the door, hoping that someone inside would unlock the door and let her in. After several attempts, she tried the handle, it moved, but did not open the door. She pulled up and down on the handle several times, but the door remained shut. Taine had told her that there were to be no witnesses to the removal of the drive, so she could not go ask about a key to get in. Stumped for a moment, she channeled Paolo, thinking about how he would bypass this obstacle. Abby pressed the lever toward the floor as hard as she could, and slammed her shoulder into the door. On the fourth slam, the door popped open, and the handle remained in her hand.

"Shit!" she said under her breath. She went into the room and closed the door almost full, and laid the handle on the desk to the right of the door. Switching the light on, Abby moved the mouse on the desk back and forth waking up the computer. There was no password screen, just a flashing cursor winking at her, awaiting some kind of entry. She keyed in the file number Taine had given her and the search box changed into an hourglass. Moments later a page expanded onto the screen. It not only contained the aisle, row, and shelf location of what she was looking for, it contained the name of the case detective who placed it into evidence.

"Richards!" she said aloud. "Sorry, I need this more than you do."

Abby clicked on the button labeled *End* and the screen went blank. She headed to the row, and aisle that the computer said held the drive. She found the shelf where the drive was supposed to be, but the entire shelf was empty.

"Shit!"

Franticly, she searched the shelf above for the drive, nothing. The same with the shelf below, still nothing. Frustrated now with the results being what they were, Abby turned in a huff and slammed her back against the shelf unintentionally. It rattled, but stopped just as fast as it started. When she calmed down, the brown file box on the self directly in front of her displayed the seven-digit alpha-numeric file number she was looking for and Richard's name in bold black marker.

Abby stood tip-toe and lifted the lid of the box, peeking inside she saw it contained only one manilla clasped envelope. She removed the lid, grabbed the envelope and put the cover back on the box. Opening the envelope, she looked inside and saw a red and black thumb drive. Taking it out, she then inserted it into the computer at the desk.

"Bingo!" she exclaimed, proud that she had found what Taine wanted. Abby removed the drive, placed it back in the envelope, and clasped it. She turned out the lights, then pulled the door open enough to peek into the hallway. Clear to her left, she opened it more and peered to the right. All clear, relief set in. she pulled the door closed and stuck the broken handle back into the hole in the door. It appeared closed, good enough she thought as she made her way to the stairs. Abby stayed as close to the wall as she could, stopping across from the bottom step, she peered up the stairs as far as she could, hesitating, not sure when to make her move. The decision was made for her as a bell

tone rang out indicating the elevator door was about to

open and let loose its cargo.

Abby moved without hesitation, envelope in hand,

to the top of the stairs and toward the small lobby that she

came through earlier. Passing several patrolmen and

detectives on the way, she smiled as she walked by them.

She could feel several of them turn and watch her leave, but

then she felt them turn back without any undue notice of

who she was or why she was there. She made it to the front

door and stopped suddenly. There, just in the middle of the

street, heading toward her and the doors, was Detective

Richards. She had to hide somewhere in a building she was

not familiar with, somewhere close to the front doors, to

escape being discovered by Richards. Just across the way

from the doors, next to the desk Sargent's station was an

open office door. She scurried inside and surprised its

occupant.

"May I help you cadet? The man in the white policeman's shirt asked.

"Oh . . . I'm so sorry Captain. I was looking for the ladies' room." She said faking surprise.

"Does this look like a ladies room cadet" the captain asked a bit perturbed.

"Again, sorry sir. I'll leave you to it" Abby said backing out and into the lobby.

She turned slowly and looked around for Richards. His back was to her as he ascended the stairs to the second floor. Abby made a bee line to the doors and out into the street. Half a block from the district building, she leaned her back against a brick wall and caught her breath.

"Damn . . . That was too close." Abby made her way to the jeep parked just around the corner from the police building. She jumped in, placed the envelope in the glove box, and sped off, heading toward home to change out of her fake uniform. She made lite of the episode as a

way to calm her nerves. "Now I can add Police Recruit to

my resumé!"

Seven

Sunday

Abby tried to rest into the morning, but her mind was on Paolo. She didn't know how he was, if he was being cared for, or if he was alive. If Taine was anything, she was a master of manipulation. She had Abby and Paolo jumping through hoops every time they were involved with each other. Not that the pair didn't try to avoid Taine at all costs, the woman always found a way to insert herself into their lives. Their longest stretch Taine-less was three months to the day, and then as the saying goes, she was on them like white on rice. Paolo and Abby knew that one day, one of the three of them would die at the hands of the other, but which would it be?

The morning hours continued to crawl, lingered in excruciating reluctance for time to move forward. Abby was due to meet Taine at Pennville "Sunday Evening" as the old woman demanded. First it was the warehouse, now it was Pennville, the old woman texted the change in destination just to mess with Abby. Nothing was a request with Taine, it was her way or no way. Abby knew much of Taine's history, how she became who she is, or what she is, and that's why Abby knew that it was fruitless to attempt to insert your own desires into Taine's plan.

By three pm Abby was frazzled and could not wait another minute to head to Pennville. She had dressed two hours ago in anticipation of the trek west across the state of Pennsylvania. Abby needed to calm herself, her normal way was to open a bottle of Yellow Tail, but she needed something a bit better. She rooted around in her night stand drawer and found an outdated prescription of an anxiety meds she had used after her first encounter with Taine. It had helped her then, with *her episodes* as Paolo called them, and she hoped that they would help her now. Downing twice the prescribed dosage without water made her gag a bit, but she recovered and hoped for some immediate relief. Some-time later, she was calm and relaxed, almost to the point of falling asleep on her bed.

Realizing she was about to nod off, Abby spoke to herself in the dresser mirror, "Fuck this. It's time!"

One and a half hours later, Abby's car idled at the main gate blocking her path to Pennville State Hospital. A man came out of the booth, unlatched the large gate and swung it open on creaking hinges. He signaled for Abby to roll down her window.

"Park There," he said as he pointed to a grassy area along the fence line. "And I'll escort you to the main building."

"Fine." Abby responded.

Doing as she was instructed, Abby backed the car into the spot, rolled the windows down, turned the ignition and left the keys in it. No one here was going to steal her vehicle, and if she needed a quick exit, she would not have to fumble for her keys along the way.

"Let's go!" the man said almost yelling at Abby. "Taine is waiting!"

"Yeah! Well . . . isn't she always." Abby said as she stepped out of the SUV placing her bag over her shoulder.

"You can leave the bag here, no one will take any of your belongings Miss Woo."

"Fine . . ." Abby said as she dropped the shoulder bag through the window onto the front seat.

"Feet apart, arms out," The short man instructed her. He ran his hands over her body, searching for weapons, his hands lingered between her legs just a bit too long for her comfort.

"Watch your hands pal!" Abby yelled at the guard as she backed away from him.

"Walk ahead of me. Head to the main building straight in front of you." As they traversed the narrow main drive, Abby kept peering back over her shoulder at the man carrying his automatic rifle as if he were expecting a battel to break out at any second. She thought of making small talk as they moved along the drive, but then realized that it would get her nowhere.

When they arrived at the main building, the man pointed at the wood and glass doors. Abby asked if Taine was inside, but the man just kept pointing.

"Asshole . . ." Abby said under her breath as she traversed the brick steps into the building. The main foyer was dilapidated, dirty, and smelled of mold. Abby called out, "Hello!"

Woods came out of the room adjacent to the main hall. "Well Miss Woo, I see you're still alive. Shame . . . In here please." The woman indicated the direction with a wave of her hand.

"Have a seat. Taine will be here soon."

"Soon! How soon?" Abby asked with inpatients.

"Knowing Taine," Woods began, "When she's damn good and ready!"

Abby sat in the antique green leather chair that faced the main hall. She kept touching her jeans pocket to make sure that the thumb drive was still in her possession. She scanned the room, taking in all there was to see. Peeling paint, fallen plaster from the ceiling, piles of paper strewn around the room, graffiti graced walls, and several bullet holes highlighted with blood spatter. The last item made her shiver.

Abby had sat there for over an hour before getting the nerve up to walk out of the room. She walked to the door marked *basement,* and when she touched the knob to open the door, memories of the past exploded in her mind. She was familiar with this place; this is where Taine had held her captive not so many months ago. Not that she knew the buildings layout intimately, but she knew what the bottom of the steps held. The path to the room where Paolo had found her after the kidnapping at Franklin Bank, and within that room, the body of her dead twin, a sister she didn't know she had until Taine's plan played out. Pushing the memory back into its place, Abby descended the stairs, making her way to that same room.

Abby walked the route on autopilot, all the while remembering everything that had happened the day Paolo came for her. She found herself facing the door to the room where she had been tied to a chair wired with explosives. Abby held back the anxiety that was creeping into her mind. She fought off the urge to vomit as she touched the knob of the antique door. With a bit of doubt, Abby turned the knob and pushed the door open. This time the room was brightly lit and as the door swung open, a voice rang out startling her out of her memories.

"I see you have found your way Miss Woo. Please come in." Taine spoke in a pleasant inviting voice. Abby did as she was asked.

"Love what you've done with the place, I mean after Paolo redecorated it for you."

"Your fiancé was a bit over dramatic with his attempted rescue of you."

"Attempted? He got me away from you, and I'm still alive." Abby reminded Taine.

"Again, you believe you and Mr. DeLuca can do anything but what I wish you to do."

"Enough chit chat," Abby said as she retrieved the drive from her pants pocket, "I got what you want."

Taine held out her hand, "I will take it now."

"Not until I see Paolo."

Taine dropped her hand to her side, turned her head and nodded. A door in the back of the room opened and two large men dragged Paolo into the light. Abby gasped at his appearance; he looked as if he had gone twelve rounds with a heavy weight boxer. Bruised, bloodied, one eye swollen shut, purple bruises on his chest under his torn shirt. The two men threw him to the ground.

Abby moved toward Paolo, wanting to comfort him, but Taine steeped between them. "The drive, Miss Woo."

Abby slapped the drive hard into Taine's wrinkled old palm, the sound echoed off the walls of the almost empty room, but the woman still blocked her path.

"Let me get to him!" Abby pleaded.

"No" was all Taine said.

"Look . . . I got you what you wanted, now let me see him." Abby demanded.

"You can see him from where you stand."

"We had a deal Taine, Paolo for the drive. Let me take him out of here and get him some help."

"Our deal . . . is not yet complete Miss Woo."

"Like hell it's not complete! You got the drive in the palm of your hand, now get out of my way or I'll . . ."

"Or you will what Miss Woo?" Taine shot back. "You have no allies here. You are not armed; therefore, your threats are empty and useless."

"I swear one day Taine . . ." Abby said irritated.

"Put him on his knees," Taine commanded her henchmen as she walked over to Paolo, pulled a revolver form her jacket pocket and held it to the side of Paolo's head, pressing it into his temple hard enough to make his head move sideways.

Abby watched in disbelief at the turn of events unfolding before her. The ancient women that stood now five feet in front of her, appeared as if she didn't have the strength to hold the gun to the head of Abby's future husband, let alone pull its trigger. But Abby knew better, she had seen first-hand the horrors that this old woman could inflict on someone and do it without a moment's hesitation. The woman known to her as Taine is the monster that lives under the bed, the one that your parents told you doesn't exist, the one they lied to you about to get you to go to sleep.

Paolo, on his knees, swaying side to side to the rhythm of the silent room, could barely keep his head up. He fought with every ounce of strength he had left to stay upright while pulling against the length of rope that now tied his wrists to his ankles. It proved to be a fruitless effort as he had only one recurring thought, "If I could just break free . . . help Abby." The front of his torn thread worn shirt was covered in blood, it ran from a cut in his forehead, down his nose, across his swollen lips to his chin before landing on the dark colored material on what was once a shirt.

He could hear the splatter of blood drops land on the saturated fabric, "Rain drops, I hear rain drops," he thought.

Abby's pain was deep at the sight of her fiancé, she felt her heartstrings being pulled to their breaking point, but she needed to stay in control just long enough to get Paolo out of this god forsaken hell hole. She had seen Paolo bruised and bloodied before, like the time he wrecked his motorcycle, but the beating he has endured by Taine's men while being held captive were three times as bad. Abby appealed to Paolo's captor as she pondered in her mind how in the hell they ended up back in this situation again, and how she was going to get him out of it.

Abby needed time to think of an out, a way to get herself and Paolo away from Taine. She repeated her argument again, and when she spoke it was with controlled anger and deep emotion.

"This wasn't our agreement. You told me that if I did everything you asked, you wouldn't kill him." Taine appeared to smile, but Abby couldn't tell the difference between the smile and the wrinkles that covered the old woman's life worn face.

"You agreed to the terms of the bargain, or if you wish, you may call it a contract between us two."

"But I didn't sign anything!"

"Sign!" Taine exclaimed. "I have no need for the formality of ink on paper! You of all people should know that, Miss Woo."

"You promised you would let us leave," Abby said as she thought she had a plan brewing in her head.

Taine shook her head in a slow side to side motion, it was a disappointing gesture directed at Abby, to scold her, or to show how a mother would be disappointed in her child for not understanding.

"When we discussed the terms of our agreement over tea, you indicated that you understood what was expected of you, and what was required of you at the end of our transaction."

"I did, I mean, I do, and I brought you what you asked for, a single damn thumb drive with God knows what's on it. Now hold up you end of the bargain and let us leave . . . like you said you would." Abby began pleading with Taine as the strength of her tone began to weaken, it began to show tiny fractures in its façade, and it was ready to crumble to dust at any moment.

Taine hit her with the beginnings of the final blows that would make her house of cards fall into total chaos,

"You left a loose end, an end which I told you was unacceptable."

"What God damn loose end?" Abby shouted! "No one knows I was there. No one saw me enter or leave the property room, or the station for that matter. And no one . . ." Abby suddenly stopped speaking as she realized what Taine was saying may be true.

"And yet there was a witness to your activity within the precinct building." Taine corrected her. "And for that reason, Miss Woo, Mr. DeLuca must die."

Abby yelled at Taine, "No!"

"Then you must complete the end of your bargain and do as I ask." Taine yelled back.

"Just tell me what the hell you want me to do Taine so we can be done with you!" Abby said as her anxiety peaked. Her heart was pounding in her chest like a bass drum booming in an empty concert hall. Tears formed but never fell as she struggled to hold herself together. Taine knew she had the upper hand, but she wanted to see how much further she could push Abby. She wanted to see if she could nudge her over the edge and make her do something she would never do under any circumstances, so she prepared the final words to push Abby into the abyss.

As Taine watched Abby struggle with her emotions, the old woman never showed any visible clues of how she was feeling. She had mastered the art of the poker face, no tells ever appeared on it. Her eye never twitched, her lips never curled, she never wiped her brow with the back of her hand, nothing, never ever, ever, to indicate what she was about to say or do. It felt like hours before either woman spoke or moved. Taine held Abby's gaze just long enough, and when Abby was about to speak, the old woman pulled the gun from Paolo's head and spoke without emotion, "I can offer you a final way out of your dilemma Miss Woo. One that will complete all business between us, forever."

Abby shuddered from the release of fear that held her, it felt like a sexual release, almost pleasurable as the anxiety drained from her chest to her toes. Her eyes glazed a bit, her pale skin flushed pink, and she let out an almost silent sigh.

"Was it good for you?" Taine remarked with a rare bit of sarcasm in her otherwise emotionless voice.

"What's the way out?" Abby needed to ask

At this point, Paolo no longer mattered. It was all about getting Abby to do the something she would never do; Taine let Abby sweat as both women remained quiet and idle, neither moved, neither spoke, time passed, and then Abby flinched.

"Christ . . . Just tell me what the hell you want me to do!"

The old woman put the pistol in her coat pocket and the weight of it pulled the cloth lower on one side of her body. It made Taine appear smaller than she was, like a child playing dress up and wearing her mother's clothes. She waved her hand in the air and the two muscle bound men picked Paolo up by the arm pits and dragged him into the room behind Taine, closing the door on act five of the poor pitiful Paolo play. The heels of his boots left tracks in the dust on the storeroom floor indicating which way he was dragged from Abby's sight. Taine wanted Abby's full attention with absolute focus on what she was about to say. Abby's inpatients got the best of her, she flinched again.

"What the fuck you want me to do Taine?"

"I want to see what you are willing to do to save the life of your fiancé."

"Like what?"

"May I ask you one question before I tell you what you will do to save your Paolo?"

"Do I have a choice?"

"No."

"Then just get on with it." Abby demanded.

"Miss Woo, *when you love someone . . . How far will you go?*"

"What?" Abby asked not understanding what the question had to do with anything. "Stop screwing with me and tell me what the hell you want me to do Taine."

Finally, Taine relented, "Just one simple task, and you are both free to go."

"Like what?" Abby said as she restrained herself from jumping forward and choking the words out of the old woman's mouth.

"Kill the witness." Taine said with no emotion.

Bamm! There it was! Taine's final challenge to Abby, kill someone to save the life of the person you love most in this world. Abby's stomach boiled at the thought of taking someone's life, it made her nauseous with a bit of I better find the bathroom fast because I'm about to lose control of my bowels. The act of taking a life was something she and Paolo always argued about. Abby says that killing is wrong no matter the situation, and she still feels strongly about that. Paolo always rebutted her statement with, "sometimes, it's kill or lose someone you care about or love forever. And then he told her one last truth, to end the discussion, "There will be that one time in your life when you don't have a choice, Abby."

All those discussions, arguments, pillow talks with Paolo about death and destruction and the biggest sin of all, murder, left Abby feeling as if there was no hope for the world. Paolo told her that there's no hope if you don't fight back, so sometimes, you must do what you think is right and then ask for forgiveness. Abby hated Paolo right now; hated him for being right. After the bank robbery and her abduction, followed by the subsequent fight for freedom that she and Paolo endured at Pennville State Mental Hospital at the hands of Taine, Paolo taught her how to fight and how to shoot, and explained that the two most important things to remember when using a weapon are, to aim center mass, and to shoot to kill.

Abby stood motionless, lost in thought and the dropping the f-bomb several times in a row in protest of Taine's desire. The words echoed in the vastness of the room, bouncing around the vacant basement and in Abby's head. When Taine move toward her, Abby came back to the present. The old woman was within arms-reach and Abby thought about reaching out and smacking her across the face with an open palm, instead, she tensed up out of fear. Taine pulled the pistol from her coat with her right hand and then grasped the barrel with her left. She extended it towards Abby without a word, offering it as if it were a gift. Thousands of thoughts ran through Abby's head about what she could do once she had her hands on the pistol. She could take the gun and kill the murdering bitch where she stands, she could shoot the old woman right in the middle of her fucking head and paint the door behind her with her brains. But then, Paolo would be killed by Taine's henchmen and Abby would still lose the battle and the war.

Abby locked her eyes on the weapon and grabbed it just above the grip and below the barrel with her thumb and forefinger. The gun was cold to the touch and Abby's facial features changed showing extreme disgust and displeasure. Once she had the weapon, Taine turned her back and headed toward the rusty door. Taine knew Abby would not kill her, at most, she would yell a few nasty words in her direction, but that was it. Once again,

Taine held all the cards, like she had before, like she always does.

"You have until midnight tomorrow, Miss Woo to eliminate the witness or . . ." Taine turned and look at Abby, "Do I need to say anything more?"

"I can't do that!"

"I'll see you when it's done." Taine said as she ended the conversation.

When the door closed behind Taine, Abby spun in circles in frustration as she placed the gun in her right hand and almost threw the pistol at the door as she came out of her spin, but she held tight at the moment of release. All that flew through the musty air of the basement room were several more cuss words and tears of frustration. She fell to her knees with the gun in her lap and held it there with both hands realizing its weight. The weapon was now an anchor and it kept her mind from drifting away from the task that

Taine told her to complete.

Eight

Monday

Outside the 6th precinct headquarters in Philadelphia's Chinatown, Abby sat on a rusted metal bench watching all of the people who entered the building across the street. One of these individuals will be the poor soul Taine sent her to kill. She sat there for several hours, waiting for the right moment to move inside. She saw Paolo's friend, Detective Richards, enter the building.   "Shit!" Abby mumbled, "Forgot about him working here."

Ten minutes after Richards entered the building, Property Officer Harding appeared. He came from Abby's left and passed within two feet of her. Abby lowered her gaze and pretended to look at something on her phone as Harding noticed her. But she was just another Chinese girl in Chinatown, he wouldn't think anything odd about an Asian girl sitting on a bench across the street for the police station. Harding abruptly turned left, crossed the street, made some small talk with the two officers standing by the door, and then went inside the building. Abby's anxiety made her feel exposed, as if Harding knew she was coming for him. Chaotic words ran through her mind, "Christ . . . All he did was look at me. He doesn't know shit" Abby thought to calm herself.

She stood and readied herself to walk into the building and do whatever she was going to do to Harding to save Paolo from certain death at the hands of Taine. She took out her cell phone one last time, opened the text screen and typed, "I did this for you Paolo, like you said, sometimes, you have no choice. I'll love you forever and always." She hit the send icon, knowing all the while that Paolo would never see the message. Dropping the phone into her purse, she walked into the street and stopped half way across with sudden pangs of guilt. Standing on the double yellow line that marked her point of no return, Abby began to have second thoughts. Her stomach churned as bile made its way into her mouth. Holding her hand over her mouth, she wanted to vomit, right there in the middle of the street for all to see. Tires screeched as car horns screamed while drivers yelled out their open windows for her to get the hell out of the middle of the road. Summoning all of her strength, she committed herself to doing what she came here to do, kill Harding.

*****

Abby hung her head like a child who had done something terribly wrong as she approached the desk where the duty sergeant sat. She stayed there several minutes in her own fantasy world until she heard the desk sergeant asking, "Are you okay ma'am? Can you tell me what you need?"

Abby mumbled some words that the officer could not hear, "I didn't understand you ma'am. Can you tell me why you are here?"

Abby grew nervous as the officer questioned her, she tightened her right hand around the shoulder strap of her bag to calm herself before replying, "I need to see Officer Harding."

"And what business do you have with him ma'am?"

Tears streamed down Abby's cheeks as she asked a second time to see the man that Taine sent her to kill, "Please . . . Get officer Harding for me. It's very important."

As the desk sergeant dialed the number, Abby slid her hand into her oversized purse and put her fingers around the guns grip, she slid her finger through the trigger guard and was ready to strike. Two minutes later Abby heard Harding approach her. He said something, she didn't respond. He said something else; she didn't move. He spoke again and this time he touched her shoulder to comfort her. Abby pulled the gun from her purse and held it at arms-length with both hands as she took two long steps away from Harding.

Some one shouted, "GUN!" as Harding stood motionless with his arms out, each about a foot away from his waist and his weapon with his palms facing upward. His stance was non-threatening. Abby's tears were flowing unchecked while thinking about killing another human being.

"I'm sorry," she said so soft that Harding could not hear her above the silence in the room.

"Ma'am, if you tell me what this is about, I can help you," Harding said with no emotion.

"You can't help me. This is the only way he'll be safe . . . I'm sorry," she repeated.

Every weapon in the room was pointing at her as someone out of view was yelling, "Put the weapon down, put the god damn weapon down or I will shoot!" repeatedly. All Abby could do was say, "I'm sorry," again and again.

Another officer to her right spoke in a quiet voice, "Ma'am, if you don't put the weapon down, I will shoot you. Do you understand?"

"I'm sorry . . . I'm sorry . . . I don't have a choice. It's the only way to keep him safe." Abby repeated.

Suddenly a voice boomed from the steps to the second floor, "No one shoot! Put your weapons down! I know this woman!" No one did what the man asked, they just stood there ready to remove the threat that had invaded their home.

Detective Richards called her name several times before she heard it, "Abby," soft and quiet at first utterance.

When there was no response, he raised his voice, and changed his tone to one of authority. "Abby . . . What the hell are you doing?" She looked away from Harding for the first time since drawing down on him.

"I have to do this Michael. She's got Paolo. You know what she'll do if I don't kill Harding." Abby shuttered with her breath.

"Shit!" Richards said.

Another officer yelled, "Put the gun down or I will fire!"

Richards yelled back, "I got this. No one shoots, she's a friend."

"Hell of a god damn friend you got there Richards," Someone in the room said.

Abby looked around the room realizing for the first time how many weapons were pointing at her, it was everyone in the room except Richards and Harding. Even the two cops outside the glass doors had Abby trained in their sights.

"I'm sorry," she said again as she readied to pull the trigger, but with an unexpected move, Richards stepped in front of Harding.

"Abby. Don't do this!"

"It's too late Michael. She will kill him if I don't. You know how she is." Abby said as sirens wailed outside of the building. Red and blue lights distracted her as Richards took a step forward. He was two steps away for Abby.

"Please Michael, Get out of the way. Let me do this . . . For Paolo!"

Richards took another step toward her, knowing that Abby would not shoot him, or anyone for that matter. But He knew that Taine could make people do things that they would never do, almost whatever she wanted them to.

Richards took the last step toward Abby; the gun barrel was pushing into the material of the body armor covering his chest. Abby looked from the tip of the barrel to Richards eyes, back to the barrel, over and over and over until the room felt like it was spinning in slow methodical circles.

"Michael . . . Please."

Richards closed his left hand around the weapon, and put his right hand on Abby's shoulder. "Give me the weapon Abby," he said only loud enough for only her to hear. She collapsed into his chest, releasing the pistol and ending the siege. He held it high in the air for everyone to see that the woman was disarmed and all were safe. The desk sergeant took the weapon from Richards freeing him to fully embrace Abby.

"Get her to my office, and get the paramedics in here, I need her coherent."

Richards knew the paramedic team that responded to the call. He knew them on a first name basis because he had served with one of the pair in Afghanistan. They owed each other their lives many times over, and they considered themselves brothers. Family ties are deep, but brotherhood is the truest kind of family two veterans could share. It was time for the detective to call in a favor so he asked Santiago to give Abby a sedative, something like the one he had given the detective that night the two of them were the only ones to survive a brutal fire fight just outside of Kandahar. They lost four of their fellow squad members on a useless foray into a village looking for a member of America's 52 most wanted. All they found was an ambush and death waiting for them. Santiago opposed the idea of the sedative because of the drug's potential side effects; however, he did what the detective asked.

"I don't like this Richards. You remember what happened last time we did this?"

"Yeah, I remember, but this is different. I need her calm; and I don't have the luxury of time."

Santiago gave the detective his famous death stare, the one that said he disagreed with the mission at hand but would do it anyway.

"Hey Abby," Santiago said as an introduction. "I'm going to give you a sedative. You're going to feel like you got hit by a car but that will only last a minute or two. After that, you'll feel like you're a step behind everyone else. If you don't want to do this, just say so.

Abby inhaled a shuddering breath in response to his question. She was still visibly shaking and she didn't answer verbally. Abby nodded her head in affirmation indicating that it was okay to inject the drug. Santiago wiped spot on her right arm with an alcohol pad in small circular motions, and with practiced ease, slipped the needle into her arm and injected the sedative into her bloodstream. She drew a deep sharp breath, her fingers tightened around the arms of the office chair causing them to turn a deep red as her eyes opened wide with an expansive expression of realization. She looked as if she had just discovered the long-lost secret to eternal life or the answer to the universal question of, is there a God?"

Abby calmed within minutes and she could talk without gasping for breath, trembling, or sobbing. Richards thanked Santiago with an embrace that showed the love a man could have for his brother, after all this time, the bond was still strong, just like the bond between him, Abby, and Paolo will hold. They were all family now, no matter what. Once Santiago was out of the room, Richards went all detective on Abby, "Give me all the details, and don't try to bullshit me, I know you well enough now."

"Taine needed me to get something for her . . . and I did. What I didn't know was that Harding saw me steal the file from the evidence room. After I brought the file to

Taine, she told me I had to kill Harding because he saw me take it," Abby said in one long breath.

"What was in the file?"

"A thumb drive, but I didn't access it enough to know what was on it that was important to Taine. I figured if she asked me if I looked at it, I could honestly tell her no and I wouldn't be lying."

As Abby spoke, her tone never changed, there was no inflection in her voice. No rise of pitch, no emotion at all. The sedative was having the effect he had hoped for. Richards stared at Abby, watching her face for any tells or any visual indications that she was lying.

"Why didn't you come to me?"

"She has Paolo . . . I couldn't take the chance she would find out that I talked to you. You know she would kill him if she knew I talked to you, Michael. She probably already knows Harding isn't dead, you know she has eyes everywhere."

"Yeah! She may already know, but."

"I can't go back there Michael! I can't watch her kill him!"

"She's not going to do anything until you are there to watch it happen, you know this whole thing is all about you Abby. Paolo is a convenience for Taine, just a pawn. He's an easy way for her to screw with you."

Richards picked up the handset of the phone on his desk, punched in a number on the dial pad, and spoke, "It's Richards, come to my office." Then he hung up without giving the recipient a chance to answer. He took his service weapon out of his desk drawer and handed it to Abby. "I want you to point it at me, when Harding walks in, you shoot him, center mass, like Paolo taught you."

"What! I can't!"

"We don't have any damn time to argue Abby! When he walks in, you shoot him dead center in the chest. When he goes down, you run as fast as you can, down the back stairs. My car is parked behind the station, take it and go to Paolo. Do you understand?"

Abby shook her head yes, but she didn't understand what was about to happen. As the door opened, Abby aimed the gun at the man who just walked in. Harding saw Richards standing there with his hands raised, and when he looked at Abby, Richards yelled at her.

"Do it! God damn it Abby, shoot him!"

In all the confusion of Harding's questions and Richards' shouting, Abby pulled the trigger and Harding went down, falling toward the corner wall of the office. Abby screamed when the gun fired, but the scream was more about how loud the bang was and less about the actual act of shooting Harding.

Richards spoke three words deliberate and one at a time, "Run . . . Now . . . Go!"

Abby dropped the gun and ran down the rear steps and out the door as other cops were running up the stairs toward the gun shot. She raced toward Richards' vehicle, jumped in, and fired it up. She pulled out of the parking spot, hitting another car and then headed west on 10th street. The driver she cut off blared his horn but Abby was already out of range of his derogatory comments. She stole a glance of herself in the rearview mirror, she saw how bad she looked in mascara that ran hours earlier, she saw her tear-stained face, she saw how sad she looked with swollen red eyes, and for the first time in her life, she saw a killer looking back at her. Abby pushed the pedal to the floor and sped toward her destination. She had no idea of a plan, no idea of what Richards was going to do, and no idea about why Taine was always screwing with her.

*****

Abby made it to her destination without being pulled over by the police, which was a miracle in itself as she drove the stolen car in such an erratic manner, that she hit several curbs and ran a few red lights on her way out of the city. The sections of Philadelphia she had to drive through to get to where she needed to be were highly patrolled high crime areas, and the police presence had been doubled of its normal patrols in preparation for the upcoming city elections.

By now and APB had to be out on Richards stolen sedan including a full description of Abby. She wondered how it would be worded, "Abhijishya Woo is wanted for the murder of Police Officer William Harding at the 6th precinct headquarters on North 11th street. She is presumed armed, and in possession of stolen police property. Anyone with information on this suspect is asked to contact the 'Tip Line' at 1-888-TIP-LINE."

Abby reminisced about all the shit she and Paolo have gone through since they met. She left a promising career as a medical professional for a possible career with the Philadelphia City Philharmonic Orchestra. Then she was kidnapped by Taine and held against her will until Paolo rescued her. He traded a computer thumb drive for her, a tiny piece of colored plastic and circuits for a human life. What value do people place on things these days? The most difficult thing for her to deal with was the death of her twin sister, one she never knew she had until Taine made sure the twin was already dead. The emotion of funeral planning that followed sent their relationship into a tailspin. Abby had blamed Paolo for her sister's death, if had just gotten there sooner . . . Maybe she'd still be alive. To cap it all off, Paolo insisted that she accompany him to Texas for the funeral of a woman she hated, a woman she thought was trying to take Paolo from her. Abby hated herself for several months after Brennan was murdered by Taine's hit woman. Brennan was Paolo's friend, there was nothing more to it than that. To make things worse, Brennan was the main reason Paolo was able to rescue her from Pennville, without her investigative abilities, Paolo may never have found her. Paolo reminded her about Brennan helping him find her. He did it matter-of-factly, in an insulting way, or so Abby thought, "She's the main god damn reason you're still alive Abby! Have some damn respect for the dead!" And now this shit! A fugitive from justice because Taine was still somehow involved in her life. "Damn Abby . . . you really fucked up your life over this guy" she said to the strange woman in the rear-view mirror.

She made a hard left into the parking lot squealing tires on the rough pavement. After turning off the ignition, she leaned across the front seat of the police car. Upon opening the glovebox, she found what she was looking for. Inside was a small caliber pistol along with an extra clip of hollow point bullets. She took the weapon and shoved it into her waistband like she was some bad-ass street thug about to make a hit. She recalled Richard's instructions as she eyed the remaining contents of the glove box, "There's a 9-mil sig in the glove compartment, don't be afraid to use it if you have to, it's small and easy to fire. Before you get out, pop the trunk and take a burner cell from my go bag. Power up the cell and then go find Paolo. I'll be there as soon as I can,"

Abby didn't know what Richards had planned, all she wanted to do was get to Paolo, and maybe, just maybe, get up the guts to "kill that old Chinese witch!" Abby glanced once more in the rear-view, she took the time to wash her face with a hand full of water from a half empty bottle she found on the front seat. She wanted to look her best for Paolo, as best she could, considering the situation that is.

The lock on the entry door to the warehouse was just a memory and it offered no resistance to anyone who wanted to get inside. Abby pushed hard on the rusted gray metal door and it moved with a deafening squeal announcing to the world that she had arrived. Once she was through the door, it swung shut on its own, squealing on its rusted hinges until it slammed home. The cavernous room was dark, but she knew her way around. She had been here twice before, and that was two times too many. Splashes of yellow light from the exterior sodium vapor fixtures filtered through the antique factory windows. Multiple panes of broken glass dotted the ten-foot-high green metal frames, others were missing entire panes casting shadows that would frighten most people, except for Paolo, he hasn't been fearful since he got her away from Pennville. That was what she owed him for, saving her life, getting her away from the crazy Chinese lady. Abby's anxiety began rumbling in like a freight train as the effects of the sedative were waning. She took three breaths to calm herself. Paolo taught her this method of breath control; he told her it had worked for him in the past. She knew exactly which part of the warehouse she needed to be in and she scampered there with a purposeful stride. She needed this to be her final showdown with Taine, needed this old woman to be out of her life once and for all. The truth about Taine though is she's Abby's bad penny. It's an old proverb, one her step-father always quoted, "She's like a bad penny, always turning up, and always unwelcome on any occasion as fate intercedes and torments you by making it appear again and again, and always coming when you least expect it or want it." As much as Abby used to believe that other saying, something like "all we have is the fate we make", she has come to realize that her step-father was the old wise man of fairy tale legend, and the things that he said, although outdated, were more often true than not.

Arriving at the inner sanctum of the warehouse and hoping it was for the final time, Abby shouted two words, "I'm here!" Her voice resonated confident and reassuring, she hoped it sounded that way to Taine and to Paolo . . . if he were listening. She didn't want to begin the final negotiation of their contract with a meek or timid sound to her voice, or have it appear as if she already thought the negotiations were over. Abby waited for half an hour without moving. She focused on the door in front of her as if she were doing a mind control trick to get Taine to come out before she was ready to. Nothing happened, not for another thirty minutes.

Abby grew tense with the metallic sound of a lock being opened from the opposite side of the rusted door. Taine was coming out to finish what she started over a week ago, and once again the woman had everything she wanted. She had Paolo, she had the thumb drive, she had the only witness to the theft of the drive dead in the morgue, and she had Abby standing in her warehouse wondering how the fuck she got where she is.

"You screwed up Miss Woo." A voice said from behind her.

Abby was right in what she told Richards. Taine knew about the screw up at the police station, about how Richards became involved with Abby's escape after she shot Harding. Taine knew Abby had the opportunity to kill Harding in the reception area of the station, and that's where Abby should have died at the hands of the police for killing one of their own. The scene repeated in her head like a syndicated TV show. Abby's voice burst from her chest, "Son of a bitch!"

Abby spun around and found Taine standing about ten feet from her. Her anxiety peeked because she realized that Taine knew every intimate detail of the encounter at the police station. The door now behind her, opened on its old hinges sending shivers of revulsion down her spine with the sound it made.

"Miss Woo, you must believe that I am a stupid old woman."

"No, I . . ."

"Officer Harding called me only moments after you left the police station."

"No way he called you! I shot him! I saw him die!"

"What you saw, Miss Woo, is what Detective Richards wanted you to see. He wanted you to witness the death of your intended target. However, it was all a ruse."

"No. He's dead. I killed him with Richard's gun." Abby howled.

"And yet he remains alive. I had hoped for a better outcome Miss Woo. I thought that once you killed Officer Harding, the police, in turn, would kill you, and of course I would have Mr. DeLuca eliminated, riding me of all of my burdens.”

“I don’t understand,” Abby said with hesitation, and then the lightbulb went on. “Harding worked for you. That’s why you wanted me to kill him. You lied about him being a witness and you manipulated me into killing him for you. You planned this whole thing; you didn’t even want the drive. You wanted Harding dead and you set me up to take the fall . . . again, like you did at the bank.”

“And the plan you made with Detective Richards to fool me into thinking that Harding was dead didn’t go as intended. Officer Harding is loyal to a fault, even after I sent someone to kill him, he called me to say that he was alive and that you were on your way here. Do you now understand why I do not trust men Miss Woo? They are vile creatures, only caring about their needs, no matter who they hurt or destroy in their hunt for glory and fame.”

A sound from behind her made Abby turn and look over her shoulder. Two thugs dragged Paolo from the room behind the door and threw him onto the dust covered floor. Taine walked past Abby as she turned and knelt next to her fiancé. "You look like shit Paolo."

"You look as beautiful as ever Abby," Paolo lied.

"Screw you!" Abby said as she smiled at her lover.

"Maybe after you get me out of this mess," Paolo joked.

Abby touched his cheek with her left palm. The feel of his warm skin on her hand reminded her of their first real kiss, it was in her kitchen after a late morning meal. She said something about an article in the paper she was reading as Paolo dried his hands on the dish towel. He walked over to the table and leaned forward placing his left hand on its flat surface. It was an innocent touch when he put his other hand on her right shoulder that ignited a fire in

Abby. She touched his hand with hers and as she did, she turned in her chair. Abby reached up and took his face in her hands and kissed him with deep passion. It was a kiss neither of them will ever forget, nor would they want to. Abby came back to the reality of the warehouse and as she did, she put her right hand on the pistol she had placed in her waistband. When she stood, she drew down on Taine.

Taine didn't think anything of it, nor did she react. She stood her ground a mere two feet in front of her thugs, and just a few feet from Abby.

"Paolo, can you walk?" Abby asked loud enough for everyone to hear. It took all of his strength to shake his head yes. "Good. Get on your feet, we're walking out of here." She said that last sentence more to Taine than to Paolo. The injured man winced in pain as he started to stand, he rose from the floor, wobbling like a drunkard after an all-night bender.

The two thugs pulled their weapons and aimed them at Abby and Paolo. "You are going nowhere Miss Woo. Not until our contract is complete."

With a slight nod of her head, one of Taine's henchmen took aim at Paolo and shot him. When the bullet hit him in the leg, he screamed in agony falling back to the floor he had just struggled to get up from. Abby yelled his name in sympathetic fear, "Paolllooo . . ."

Abby grabbed the pistol tighter with both hands, her face twisted in anger and in her mind, she was aiming the Sig Sauer 9mm harder at Taine, as if you could do something like aim harder at someone. Paolo growled in pain as the blood leaked through his fingers as he tried to stem the flow, the sound escalated from a low grunt to a deafening roar. He bit his lip to keep himself conscious, taking a breath he yelled with all he had at the woman he loved, "Fucking shoot her Abby!"

She knew he was angry; she had seen this side of him only once before, it was the last time the three of them stood together in a room all too similar to this one. Abby grimaced, trying to concentrate at a high level as tears blurred her vision and obscured her intended target and her judgement. She shivered with fear thinking Paolo was going to die today because she couldn't do what he told her to do. As Abby thought about taking action, Taine held out her hand palm up and one of her men gave her his weapon. She walked up and stood with her toes against Paolo's ribs, digging the tip of her shoe into his side while putting the weapon to his forehead. She pushed and in response, he moved his head to the floor attempting to gain some distance between his head and the barrel of the gun.

"Say goodbye to your fiancé Miss Woo," and as Abby's last name was spoken, two shots rang out and the two thugs with Taine fell dead to the floor. The velocity of the rounds had knocked both men backward, away from the small group inhabiting the warehouse.

"Bout time you showed up Richards!" Paolo said.

"Traffic, was all Richards said in response as he walked out of the shadows and aimed his weapon at Taine's head. The old woman looked at Richards without fear, daring him to shoot.

"Drop the weapon or I will kill you." He demanded.

Taine did as she always does, never trusts what any man says. She shook her head in disgust at his words and attempted to pull the trigger. Richards yelled, "No!" But before the word was out, a shot echoed off the cavernous ceiling of the warehouse, time stopped with a second shot echoing as the first had.

Moments later, Taine dropped, grabbing her bloody shoulder as she fell first to her knees, and then to the floor. Paolo grabbed his left ear reacting to the explosion that just occurred next to his head. Richards looked at Abby who was still holding her breath after finding the courage to shoot Taine.

"Abby . . . Abby . . . She's down. Are you okay?" The young woman dropped the pistol, and it clattered on the wooden floor. She knelt next to her boyfriend, never answering the question. Taking him in her arms she cried in relief, "It's finally over."

Richards dialed 911 on his burner cell and identified himself, "This is Detective Michael Richards badge number one niner five five, I have two civilians with gunshot wounds at 4242 West Race Street, they are in need of emergency medical services. Requesting ambulances and police back up."

After the paramedics loaded Paolo into one of the ambulances, and the old woman into the other, Taine waived her hand at Abby. Calling her over. With reluctance, she half-stepped over to see what the old woman could possibly want from her.

"What?" was all Abby said with deep disregard for the woman's condition.

"After all I have done to you, you could still not kill me," Taine spoke in a solemn motherly voice. Then it changed to one of scolding disrespect, "You have learned nothing, you are weak, Miss Woo."

The paramedics slammed the double doors of the vehicle shut and drove off with sirens wailing. Abby watched Taine's Ambulance leave to take her to Eden General Hospital, and when the vehicle was far enough down the road for Abby to be sure that Taine could not hear her words, she screamed at the rear of the vehicle in a self-comforting act of defiance, "Yeah, well not as weak as your fucking tea!"

"Miss . . . Miss, we ready to leave," The other paramedic said. "If you're coming with us you can ride up front with the driver."

Abby walked backwards toward the waiting ambulance, watching the distant lights of Taine's ambulance fade into the horizon, "Yeah, I'm coming," Abby yelled to the man in white and blue. When she got in, the driver pulled out of the warehouse parking lot, flipped on the sirens, and turned right.

"Where you taking us?" Abby asked unsure of the direction the driver was heading.

"Eden General."

"But . . ." Abby stopped mid thought and turned around as much as she could while still wearing the seatbelt. She looked toward the driver and asked the question that should have been obvious to him, "Where's the other guy going?"

"Should be going to Eden," he said. "Mercy is on by-pass, so . . ."

"Shit!" Abby interrupted.

■■

When they arrived at the emergency entrance, the paramedics announced Paolo's condition to awaiting staff. Abby followed the group as far as she could, once they reached the operating room, they held her back and escorted Paolo inside. She whispered to him, hoping that he would survive another surgery. "Love you baby . . ."

An intake person escorted Abby to a room marked family/private and had her sit on a comfortable couch. The room was adorned with everything one may need to endure a lengthy stay while your family member was undergoing surgery. The rep took all of Paolo's personal information that Abby could provide, and the asked her if she were thirsty or wanted something to eat.

"Water," Abby said

The woman handed her a bottle of water marked with the Eden General logo, and then told her that if she needed anything, anything at all, to use the phone on the table and simply ask for it.

"Okay," Abby said as the woman left the room leaving Abby totally alone. Abby lost her control and broke down in tears, sobbing as if she were never going to see Paolo again. She grabbed a pillow off the couch and buried her face into its cold antiseptic surface. Abby screamed several times, crying, breathing, shaking uncontrollably until she had let all of the pent-up emotion of the past days loose from her body. She put the pillow on the arm of the couch, laid her head on it and her feet on the cushion. She fell asleep in seconds, exhausted from life itself.

Abby awoke to someone calling her name, "Abby . . . Abby sweetheart, wake up."

"Daddy?"

"I'm here baby. Mother is her too." Her father said.

Abby cried again, this time in her father's arms. Like she had so many times as a child. Both parents, now on the couch, hugged their daughter, held her until she calmed enough to talk.

"How's Paolo?" Abby asked.

"No word yet," her mother said. "But if we don't hear something soon, I'll go light a fire under that woman in registration."

As they made small talk, Detective Richards knocked, opened the door, and asked if it was okay to come in.

"Please, sit with us Detective," Abby's father said.

"Please, call me Michael."

"Liron," Her father said.

"Leon?" Richards asked.

"Ahh, close enough," the man told him.

"Michael, sit next to me," Abby Said, and when he did, she whispered, "I don't think Taine's here. Her Ambulance went somewhere else."

"Yeah, I checked at intake. She's not here. I have someone checking other hospitals, but I'm sure she's not in any of them."

"That fucking bitch got away . . ." As Abby spoke her mother expressed her displeasure.

"Abhijishya Woo!" Her mother said. "Mind your tongue."

"Sorry mom. It's just . . ." Then her father laughed and said "That's my girl!"

Nine

One Week Later

Paolo was due to get out of the hospital today, a full week after being admitted, again, to Eden General. He had been here so often, everyone that worked in the ER knew him on a first name basis. Most of them could recite his chart verbally without glancing at it, and the head of the ER department told him to just put in a job application at HR since he was here so often. "We could use a good ER clean up guy. The pay sucks, but the benefits are great, and you probably won't get shot here."

"Thanks for the offer, Doc, but I got all the work I can handle." Paolo shot back.

Abby came in as the pair were finishing up their conversation. She hugged Paolo and greeted the doctor with a friendly smile.

"Abby, can you take this guy home and get him out of my hair . . . once and for all?"

"Cars waiting! All we need is a set of wheels to get him downstairs."

"I'll finish his discharge papers and order the chair. DeLuca, hope to never see you again."

"Same to you Doc!"

The orderly arrived and assisted DeLuca into the chair. He took them both to the front entrance and assisted him into the SUV. Abby's dad welcomed him with a big smile and an enthusiastic pat on the shoulder. "Welcome home son!" the man exclaimed.

Abby got in the back seat behind Paolo. She reached up and touched his shoulder just as her father had. Let's go home baby."

"Drive already!" Paolo shouted back.

They all had a good laugh and soon the vehicle grew quiet. It stayed that way until it pulled into Abby's driveway. The pair helped Paolo out of the car, but he insisted walking up the drive to the front door. He looked at his new SUV as he passed it and stopped dead in his tracks.

"What the hell?"

"Sorry Paolo." Abby said, "didn't see the brick pier until I hit it."

"Don't ever drive my car again Abby . . ."

She teased back at him. "Still gotta ferry your lame ass around until you can drive yourself."

I can always Uber...."

*****

Two weeks had passed since Paolo was discharged from Eden General Hospital. He started rehab at the local facility, but he didn't interact well with any of the therapists. He was passed from therapist to therapist, as if he were a yesterday's news. No one was interested in helping a man who thought he knew better than they did.

Finally, they asked him to leave and the head therapist gave him the address of a local establishment where he may fit in.

"This place caters to vets, especially the difficult ones, like yourself, Mr. DeLuca. I called ahead they are expecting you."

"Thanks for nothing." Paolo shot back knowing this was all his doing. He headed to the new facility to sign up for services, but half way there his cell rang.

"Yeah?" was all he said.

"How you feeling brother?" Richards said. "You making out okay?"

"Same old shit Richards."

"In other words, they made you go somewhere else."

"They did." Paolo confirmed.

"Listen, got some more bad news. Got a lead on Taine. My CI says she's held up in a place you're all too familiar with."

"Let me guess, Pennville . . ." Paolo said less as a question and more as a fact.

"Yeah. Waiting for a judge to sign a warrant for Out-of-County Enforcement. Should have it by this time tomorrow. You up for a trip?"

"I'm in. What about Abby?"

"Best to keep her safe. Keep her away from Taine and Pennville, especially since she still hasn't found anything on her sister's body."

"I'll let her know the details. But she's not going to like not being able to tag along."

"You sure you want to tell her?"

"New rules Michael, no secrets, no matter how hurtful they may be."

"Good luck with that. I got authorization for you as a ride along. Be here at eight sharp."

"Anyone else going? Watts maybe?"

"Watts is on leave. The commissioner didn't like the outcome of the last go-round at Pennville, let alone Abby's attempt on the life of a police officer in our own house, even on a piece of shit like Harding."

"Extenuating circumstances Richards. You know how Taine is. Bitch is a master at manipulation." Paolo reminded his friend.

"Yeah, she's a piece of work. Listen, eight o'clock, no later."

"Roger that. One more thing. I have something else I need to tell you about, but it's best to do it in person."

"Serious?"

"Could be. Just can't hold it back any longer."

"I'm intrigued. See you in the a.m." And with that Richards disconnected the call.

Paolo forgot about his appointment with the VA rehab facility and made a quick U-turn to head to Abby's place. He figured, better to not put this off, or she'll be all up in his face about secrets and promises, again.

Ten

Encounter

DeLuca pulled up to the call box at the sixth district police precinct building. He pressed the call button and waited several minutes. Finally, a voice came over the box.

"Sir this lot is for police vehicles only. You'll have to park on the street, if you need assistance, come to the front desk. Someone there will help you."

Paolo spoke at the silver grille on the gray metal box. "I'm Paolo DeLuca. I'm here to meet Detective Richards for an eight o'clock."

"Just a moment please." Then the voice came back on. "Richards said for you to park along the back fence and he'll meet you there. Back your vehicle in along the fence line and wait in your vehicle until Detective Richards meets you there. Do you understand my directions sir?"

"Yes, I do."

With that, the metal chain link gate opened on its own, grinding and scraping with screams of ungreased agony as it traveled its path.

Paolo pulled through and the gate repeated its song in the opposite direction, closing in the vehicle as if it were a fly in a spider's web. Paolo saw Richards come out of the door marked Police Personal Only, and head toward his SUV. He got out and Richards greeted him with unceremonious words. "Ready to go?"

Paolo hung his head. "Guess we are."

"We?" Michaels asked.

And with that, Abby opened the passenger door of the SUV and jumped out.

"God dammit DeLuca! I told you she couldn't come."

"Wasn't my choice Richards."

"Don't talk about me like I'm not part of this Michael. Paolo told me no, yet here I am."

"I only got authorization for DeLuca, you can't . . ."

Abby shut him down without a word. She got into the back seat of his police sedan and buckled the seat belt. As she pulled the door shut as she yelled at her two companions, "Let's get this show on the road."

"Guess she's coming along." Richards said.

"Was there any doubt?" DeLuca asked rhetorically.

*****

The forty-five-minute drive to the Pennville facility took an hour and a half due to construction traffic. All of the occupants of the sedan were growing agitated with the snail's pace of the traffic through the lanes which were barricaded like cattle chutes. Cars had no exit options and no switch lane options. All they could do was follow the car in front of them until the end of the construction zone.

In a way, the cattle chutes were a representation of Abby's life since she had become involved with Taine. No way out until the end, had to follow the course set for you by someone other than yourself. Abby didn't know what Richards had planned to do after he served his warrant, but she had her own plan, confront Taine for the final time. End this forced marriage once and for all.

Upon arrival at Pennville, and as Richards drove his sedan toward the main entry gate, the man at the gate opened it and waved them through without having to be told.

"Guess Taine is expecting us." DeLuca said.

"I'm sure someone at the precinct alerted her to the warrant being issued." Richards said in response.

"Probably that jackass Watts." Abby interjected.

"Watts could not have said anything, besides . . ." Richards began.

Abby interrupted his outburst, "You didn't tell him?"

Paolo spoke up. "About that." He reached into his pocket and held up the red and black thumb drive as if it were more bad news.

"What the hell is that, DeLuca?"

"It's the original drive, like the one I gave you at the station. Except there is one additional file I didn't copy for you. Thought I could save you some trouble."

Richards grabbed the file out of DeLuca's hand like a bully snatching candy from his foil. "How about you let me decide what the hell kind of trouble I can handle. Christ DeLuca, I don't give a shit about Watts. He's been nothing but a pain in my ass since this Taine thing started. So, what the fuck is on here that wasn't on the last drive?"

DeLuca took a deep breath before explaining as the sedan arrived at the main building at Pennville. "A file on the sixth district. It has all of the names in it that Taine owns within the district. It also contains monetary amounts paid out, dates paid, and links to open cases that she must have an interest in. Shit like that."

"We'll deal with this later." Richards said as he got out of the sedan.

Paolo and Abby followed as Richards explained the process of how this would go down. "You two are here to observe, nothing else. Do you read me DeLuca? Abby?"

Roger that." DeLuca responded. Abby didn't say a word, she just followed along thinking how this was going to be the final conflict in their long battel. All she really wanted was the location of her sister's body, nothing else.

As they ascended the steps to the wood and glass front entry doors, the one on the right opened and a man invited them into the room that lay just off the main entry hall. The same room Paolo had been in with Su Anne, and the same room Abby had been in when she came to get

Paolo away from Taine.

"This déjà vu shit has got to stop." Abby said in

disgust as she scanned the room looking for Taine or

Woods.

Just as Richards was about to comment, Woods

walked in and announced that Taine would receive them as

a group."

"Let me do this the professional way." Richards

said. "I have a warrant to search the premises, including all

buildings, sheds. Out houses, and any other structure on

this property. Also, I have a warrant for the arrest of the

woman known as Taine."

Woods chuckled at the policeman's statement.

"Good luck with that detective. Now if you'll follow me."

The woman turned and headed toward the basement. The

same basement Taine had been in before, the same

basement Paolo and Abby had both been before, too many times for either one of them to want to remember fondly.

They walked the long hallway to the last door as they had the last several times, they all had been here. Woods opened the door and stood aside as the three of them entered the mostly vacant room.

"Have a seat, Taine will be here . . . well, you know, when she's damn good and ready." Woods told them.

None of them sat. They all just stood in silence until the door at the back of the room opened and a man in scrubs pushed Taine toward them in a wheel chair, complete with an IV drip and an oxygen bottle.

The trio regrouped and stood in a semicircle facing Taine.

"Taine, I have a warrant for your arrest in the murders of . . ." Richards began.

"Yes, yes. Detective Richards. I know all about your warrant. Captain Watts informed me of your pending arrival before I had him removed."

"Removed?" Richards asked.

"Would you rather I say something else? Perhaps another word for disposed of, or eliminated."

"You had him killed." DeLuca stated.

"In truth, Mr. DeLuca, I sent Miss Woods to eliminate him, but he chose to do the task himself, rather than allow her the pleasure." Taine told the trio.

Richards dialed his cell, calling the desk sergeant to inform them of this information. "Yeah, this is Richards. Get someone over to Watts house. See what the hell is happening over there."

He listened to the voice on the other side of the conversation and then disconnected. "Watts is dead. Patrol found him a half hour ago."

"I have no reason to lie to you Detective. Captain Watts was another loose end I needed tied up before this all ends." Taine said as Woods joined her by her side.

"It's over Taine." Richards said as he began to mirandize the old woman.

"And yet, it is not." Taine said in return as Woods and the man in scrubs pulled weapons on the three facing Taine.

Richards and DeLuca both drew their weapons and aimed them at the group on the other side.

"Well, it appears we are at a draw." Taine said.

"No, we're not." Richards said as he opened fire and took down both Woods and the man in scrubs. The man died instantly, Woods was bleeding from a wound to her shoulder and was reaching for her weapon with her good hand. This time, Richards took careful aim and put a bullet in Woods forehead. Threat neutralized.

Taine had also drawn her own weapon. As she lifted it to aim at the group, DeLuca shot her, hitting her in the shoulder of the hand that held the weapon. As this unfolded, Richards called for backup, state and local police would arrive in a matter of minutes.

Abby ran up to Taine and pressed on the wound to stem the flow of blood, not wanting Taine to die before she found out the location of her sister's body.

"Where is Abhijaya's body? And where is Su Anne?"

"There is no body." Taine said.

"What did you do with her?" Abby said getting angry.

"I have done nothing, Miss Woo." Taine corrected her.

Abby picked up the gun from Taine's lap and held it to the old woman's head. "Tell me where she is or so help me Taine. . ."

Taine spoke at Abby again like a mother to an arrogant child. "You cannot kill me, Miss Woo. As much as you hate me, you will never be able to kill me. Remember . . . last time?"

Abby knowing this was the truth, moved the gun from Taine's head to her knee and to the surprise of all in the room, pulled the trigger.

Taine winced in pain but never called out. When the pain passed, Taine spoke. "You are not the innocent girl you once were, Miss Woo."

"No, I'm not." Abby said as she moved the weapon to Taine's other knee and pressed it into the skin.

"Now tell me where my sister and Su Anne are."

Taine stared at Abby with no intent of revealing anything. Abby fired the weapon again and Taine winced in pain, but never cried out. Paolo intervened.

"Abby, let me finish this."

On the verge of tears, Abby stood and backed away as Paolo replaced her threat with his own. "Tell me where they are Taine, and I'll get the paramedics here to help you, or I can just kill you now and we'll find them on our own."

"No need, Mr. DeLuca. My time is at an end. There is a key in my pocket, it will unlock the door behind me. You will find what you seek there." Taine said gasping as she struggled to hold on to life as long as she could.

DeLuca searched Taine's pockets until he found what he was searching for. He gave the key to Richards who unlocked the door. He went in with his weapon trained on whatever threat may come. From within the room, Richards called out. "Abby, get in here."

Abby did as she was told. She ran across the basement room, through the door, and stopped within two feet of Richards. There, tied together, sitting on the floor blindfolded, gaged, and frightened were Su Anne and Abhijaya, both alive.

Abby and Richards untied the pair, Abby cried as she hugged her sister who returned it with her own tears. Su Anne stood with the help of Richards. "Where's Taine?" The girl asked obviously in pain from the scars and contusions visible on her face and neck.

"Who did this to you?" Abby asked the girl.

"That bitch Woods, kept beating me because I wouldn't do what she wanted me to. Where is Taine, is she still here?"

"In the other room. She's badly wounded, probably not gonna make it."

Su Anne ran from the room ahead of the others and found Paolo dressing Taine's wounds, trying to stop the bleeding. He looked at the girl. "Glad you're safe Su Anne."

"We're not safe yet, not as long as Taine is alive. I was hoping one of you had killed her." She said.

Paolo felt a deep despair at the thought of a girl so young wishing for the death of a much older woman, but he understood why. Taine had put this girl through hell in just the short time that he and Abby had known her. No one that young, or any age for that matter, should have to deal with Taine's abuse.

Abby came to the conversation late, but she knew the gist of it. "Paolo, take Su Anne and Abhijaya outside. Leave Michael with me. I need to talk to Taine." Paolo didn't question Abby's wish he just did as he was asked. When the three were out of the room, Abby knelt by

Taine's side and looked at the old woman remembering all that she had done to her and her fiancé. She had one question she needed Taine to answer, "Why?"

"It was nothing personal Miss Woo. As I have told you in the past, you, your sister, DeLuca, Richards, Brennan, all of you were just a means to an end."

"And Su Anne?"

"Hope . . . for the future."

"To carry on your legacy?"

"Yes. To do unto others . . . before they do unto you."

"And that gave you the right to screw with our lives? To fuck with us any time you saw fit?"

"I have no regrets, Miss Woo. I know what I was, and most importantly, why I was."

"I feel no sympathy for you Taine, and when you are dead, I will not think of you again."

"But you will, Miss Woo. I will always be a part of you. You will think of me often, perhaps not in such a pleasant way, but always. If you doubt me, ask your fiancé about the ghosts he still carries for the good he did for his country. We are more alike than you care to admit."

"I am nothing like you, Taine."

Taine and Abby looked at each other for many moments before Taine spoke again. "Miss Woo, there is one more thing I wish you to have." The old woman said as she reached into her jacket pocket. Abby was a bit startled when she saw the old woman take the knife from her pocket. "Take this knife and keep it with you. It has always brought me luck, and it has saved my life on many unpleasant occasions." Taine held the knife by its blade as she waited for Abby to take it. "It is my only true possession, Miss Woo. I want you to have it."

"No! I don't want the damn thing. How many people have you killed with it?"

"Too many to remember." Taine said as she grabbed Abby's wrist and slapped the blood-stained wooden end into the palm of Abby's right hand. Abby tried to pull away and was surprised at how strong Taine still was in her weakened state. As Abby tried to pull away, Taine grabbed her wrist with both hands and forced Abby to put the knife to her throat. The sharpness of the tip of the blade caused a trickle of blood to ooze from Taine's neck.

"You must end this here, Miss Woo, end it now."

Abby struggled hard but could not get loose of Taine's grip. "Let me go. I am not like you. I just can't kill someone." Tears began to flow from her eyes.

"All that I have done to you, and you still disappoint me. All that I have taken from you, and you will not take revenge. I held you captive, placed you on top of an explosive device, kidnapped your fiancé, kept you and your sister apart for many years. And your adoptive parents . . ."

"What about them?"

"If I am seen outside of this room, Miss Woo, they will be killed before you get home to them.

Abby was in full tear mode, almost hysterical. Crying as she cussed at Taine. "Please, tell me you are lying . . . tell me you did not send someone to hurt them . . . or kill them."

"Only you can end this, Miss Woo."

Abby tried again to pull away, but Taine was much too strong for her to break the iron like grasp on her wrists. When Taine spoke again, it was in a different voice.

"Please, Abby, set me free."

And then just as suddenly as the voice appeared, it changed back to Taine's usual tone and inflection. "You can set Lien Bo free, Miss Woo."

Taine let go of Abby's wrist with her right hand and placed it on Abby's left cheek. It was a warm moment of tenderness that Abby didn't expect. "You look so much like my daughter."

Abby was taken aback. No one knew Taine had a daughter, and the news of this to Abby, made her relax her arm, the arm holding the knife. Taine felt the tension dissipate, and grabbed Abby's wrist again with both hands. She plunged the knife into her own throat guaranteeing her death.

Abby screamed in response, *"NNNNOOOOOOOO!"*

Richard's witnessing the entire exchange, pulled Abby up and away from Taine. The old woman died in mere seconds, eyes open, staring directly at Abby no matter where she stood in the room. Richard's led Abby outside, passing the police and EMT's at the top of the stairs.

"Basement room." Was all he said to them.

Paolo, Abhijaya, and Su Anne ran to the pair when they came out the front door of the main building. Abby was still crying, almost incoherent, still carrying the knife in her hand. Paolo and Abhijaya didn't notice the weapon until Su Anne spoke.

"That's Taine's knife!"

"What the hell happened down there?" Paolo said.

"Taine's dead. She forced Abby to kill her."

Abby came out of her stupor at the sound of her name. She hugged Paolo, sobbing uncontrollably, still holding the knife as it dripped Taine's blood onto Paolo's back. He spoke softly into his fiancée's ear. "Abby, let me have the knife. I'll get rid of it, bury it somewhere."

Abby let Paolo out of the hug as she spoke back to him. "No. She gave it to me." Abby said as she put the knife into her back pocket. He moved Abby, her sister, and Su Anne toward the waiting ambulances. EMT's looked over the group and decided to take Su Anne to Eden General for a follow up examination since she had been beaten so badly. Abby and Abhijaya rode in the ambulance with Su Anne, Paolo told them that he would meet them there with Richards when they were done at Pennville.

Richards saw that the Deputy Commissioner of the Philadelphia Police department was on site. "Got one thing to do DeLuca. Stay by the car. I got to talk to Salazar."

Paolo watched from a distance as Richards talked and Salazar listened. Richards held up the thumb drive and Salazar pulled it from his hand. There was a lot of finger wagging in Richard's direction, as well as some fingers to Richards chest. When the blame game ended, Richards returned to his sedan and DeLuca.

"Didn't look like he was too happy with you Richards." DeLuca said to his friend.

"Same old shit DeLuca, and a ton of paperwork to fill out."

"We outta here?" DeLuca asked.

"Yeah. Let's get to the hospital. I need to take statements from everyone. Got to make the boss happy." The pair rode to the local hospital in silence. When they got there, and before they got out of the sedan, Richards spoke to DeLuca.

"Here's what went down DeLuca, Woods and Taine had words about how to eliminate the three of us. They argued, Woods grabbed Taine's knife and killed her. In response, I shot Woods twice. That's it. That's all you guys will remember. You go talk to them. Tell them what to say. Nothing else. All of you stick to the same story and you'll be fine."

DeLuca didn't respond. He met up with Abby, Abhijaya, and Su Anne. Abby hugged him when he arrived and filled him in on Su Anne's condition.

"They are keeping her overnight, but she's okay otherwise. "Great news, but I'm sure she'll need some counseling."

"The four of us need to talk about Pennville." Richards said.

"Why?" Abby began. "It's done, Taine is dead."

"True" Paolo added. "But we need to get the details right. I'm sure the people in charge are going to want to interview all of us."

"Yes, they will" Richards added.

Eleven

Three Months Later

It had been weeks since Abby had thought about Taine, Pennville, and all the investigations and interviews that had gone down since that final day at the Pennville facility. Abby and Abhijaya had rekindled their sisterhood and were as close as sisters could be. They told each other their life stories since they were separated on the day of their birth. Su Anne was a regular visitor at the Woo home. In fact, Abhijaya and Su Anne were roommates at a rental property not far from Abby's house. Su Anne was going back to school and Abhijaya had a full-time job in the records department at the sixth district headquarters building, thanks to Richards who had been promoted to Captain after the final take down of the Philadelphia Triad. His promotion was a reward for standing tall in the face of adversity, not only with Taine, but with the corruption he uncovered within the Philadelphia police department.

On the final Friday of the month, exactly three months to the day of their final showdown with Taine at Pennville, Abby, her sister, Su Anne, Paolo, and Richards were finishing up dinner at the Woo home. Abby's parents had just arrived with desert and were ready to sit down and enjoy a long night of conversation and coffee with this new family group. As they chatted about the miracle of the reunification of Abby and Abhijaya, there was a knock at the door.

"I'll get that Abby, if you cut me another piece of that delicious apple crumb cake."

Su Anne came back to the kitchen several moments later. "Abby, the guy at the door says he's from Rosendorn and Abramowitz law firm. He says it's important and will only talk to you." She handed Abby a business card.

Abby read the card, "What the hell is this about?" She said to no one in particular as she headed for the front door.

Abby opened the door and asked the man "What's this about?"

"Miss Woo, if I may come in, out of the rain," the man said as he looked skyward, "I can give you all of the details."

Abby let the man inside and shut the door behind him. When he looked up, everyone in the house was looking at him, wondering what was going on.

"Ah . . . Good! You are all here. That will make my job a bit easier." The man said to all.

"What's this about?" Paolo asked as he stepped forward a bit enraged.

The man held up his hand and spoke softly with no threat in his voice. "If we can sit somewhere and discuss this business, I am sure you'll understand in no time why I am here."

The group adjourned to the living room. Everyone took a seat as Paolo brought a dining room chair for the lawyer to sit on. The man thanked him and placed his brief case on his lap. He opened it and took out a file, almost as thick as the case itself. Out of the file he handed Abby, Abhijaya, and Su Anne a white business envelope with their full legal names on it.

"I will begin as you three open these documents." He said not wanting to prolong his intrusion into their evening.

"First, I am sorry for my late arrival. All of this business of the legality of this procedure just finished at city hall this afternoon."

Abby had opened her envelope and spoke first. "Is this for real?" She said as she handed the document to Paolo to read.

"Yes, Miss Woo. I can assure you that it is. If I may, I can brief you on the contents of all of the letters, beginning with the three of you, and then Mr. DeLuca and Captain Richards."

Stunned into silence, Abby spoke for the group a bit angry, and a bit surprised. "You got three minutes, before I toss you out." The group looked on in wonder at what was about to unfold.

"Miss Woo, again I apologize for the late hour; however, this must be done before midnight tonight or everything reverts to Taine Enterprises which then will be dispersed to the city for dissolution. You can imagine how that will go, and, if I may say, what a waste it would be."

"Get on with it. You're wasting time." Abby said as Paolo showed the paper to Richards.

"As stated in your copies of the documents, Taine has left each of you what is described within each of the individual letters. Miss Kang will inherit the Rising Sun hotel and funding to keep it in good repair, to include taxes and whatever bills arise until she reaches the age of twenty-five. Then she will inherit the sum of one million dollars to use at her discretion. Miss Abhijaya Woo, will be given the sum of five million dollars and all warehouses once owned by Taine. If she wishes to sell the ten properties, all funds of the sale will be given to Abhijaya in their place."

The group sat in silence at the lawyer's announcement. "To continue, Miss Abhijishya Woo will receive five million dollars and the tract of land known as Pennville as well as any monies needed for costs of upkeep of the property."

Abby protested. "I don't want anything from that woman."

"Miss Woo, if you let me finish with this presentation, there will be an opt out clause for each of you."

Abby shook her head if affirmation for him to continue. "Mr. DeLuca, you are to obtain ownership of the tract of land at the former navy yard where your warehouse once stood to do with as you wish. There are interested parties in purchasing the land for development if you wish to go that route. And finally, Captain Richards. Since it may be deemed inappropriate for you to inherit money from Taine, you are to receive a collection of firearms once owned by Taine, again if you wish they can be sold at auction as they are worth several thousands of dollars."

Abby spoke again, "I don't know about the rest of you, but I don't want her blood money."

"As I said, there is an opt out clause in the contract if you wish to go that route. All monies from Taine and from the sale of all of her holdings will be given to an investment group overseen by myself and my partners. The money will be used to build a center for the benefit of everyone in Chinatown. Again, it is your decision, but I need these documents signed by midnight, either way."

Abby asked the man one last question. "Why did she leave any of this to us? It's not like we are related."

The lawyer snapped the latches on his briefcase shut and placed it on the floor next to him. He took a deep breath before he spoke.

"Taine told you the story of how Chang Lo killed her daughter just after the child was born . . ." he began.

"Yeah. Old news." Abby said with deep sarcasm.

"Well, what she didn't tell you was that she tracked down all of the women in the room at the time of the birth.

Lien Bo had given birth that day, as she had told you, but she didn't know until years later that she had given birth to twin girls. The women in the room had hidden the second child from Chang Lo to save her life. They took her out of the room moments before Chang Lo came in. Not even Lien Bo knew of the second child until Taine was already in America."

"And what does this have to do with my sister and me?" Abhijaya asked the man who appeared to be stalling the story as if he didn't want to reveal a secret.

"Taine tasked my firm to track down any information on the other child. We found some evidence, although it is spotty at best, of ties to both Miss Woo's.

"What kind of ties?" Abby asked, afraid of what the answer was going to be.

The man took in a deep breath as he loosened his tie. "We feel, with the information we found with the help of the Chinese government, and several DNA testing facilities, that there is a ninety percent chance that Lien Bo was your Great Grandmother."

Paolo spoke up for the group as they were all stunned into silence. "Give us some time, to talk this over."

"I can return at 11 p.m. It will take some time to sign all of the documents, whichever way you choose to go."

At 11 p.m. the doorbell rang and Abby let the lawyer in. They took up their seats as they had before. "Well, what have you decided to do?" The lawyer asked.

Abby spoke for the group. "Su Anne will go along with the agreement that you proposed for her. Abhijaya will only agree to a monthly stipend for the rest of her life if you put all of the funds toward the Chinatown center. The rest of us, we agreed to opt out entirely, as long as all funds whether it be cash or money from the sale of properties goes to the center. None of us want anything else from the witch."

"Understood." Was all the man said in return as he pulled a final document from his brief case. He made some changes to the papers, signed his name as representative of Taine's estate and had each of the group involved sign the papers.

"Miss Su Anne, Miss Abhijaya, I will bring your copies of the paperwork by tomorrow morning. Funds for your use will be deposited into you accounts as soon as you provide us with your banking information. Miss Woo, Mr. DeLuca, Captain Richards, I will process these documents tonight and contact the necessary parties to begin the planning and construction of the center. There are only two last stipulations before this agreement is finalized Miss Woo."

"Of course, there are." Abby said "Taine always has to have the last word. What are they?"

"Simple really." The Lawyer began. "The first is that you and Mr. DeLuca must agree to sit on the board of trustees for the new center through its construction and continued operation."

"And what's the second?" Abby asked already suspecting the answer.

"We must all sit and have a cup of tea as we sign the agreement."

"Well, what's one more cup of tea among friends? Su Anne, would you like to do the honors?" Abby spoke to all in the room, "We'll do it for Lien Bo, not for that other woman."

The End

Other Books by Paul Toritto

Abby Woo

The Book of Taine

A Cup of Tea

Opus 22, The short story, Father John

Frightful Tales of All Hallows Eve. The Day of All

Hallows' Eve (Drabble)

Thank you to all who have given their

support and encouragement during this

adventure! It is truly appreciated.

www.ingramcontent.com/pod-product-compliance
Lightning Source LLC
Chambersburg PA
CBHW060404310726
48976CB00003B/937